A DIFFERENT KIND OF LOVE

AND OTHER STORIES

BY

JAY MANDAL

BeWrite Books, UK
www.bewrite.net

Published internationally by BeWrite Books, UK.
363 Badminton Road, Nibley, Bristol, BS37 5JF.

British Library Cataloguing in Publication Data.
A catalogue record for this book is available from the British Library

ISBN 1-904224-40-7

Also available in eBook and cd-rom formats from www.bewrite.net

Digitally produced by BeWrite Books, UK.

Original cover photography by Skovia Grassi

"We probably went about it in completely the wrong way."

"What d'you mean?"

"Well, maybe we should simply have done what everyone else does."

"But could you? Wouldn't you find it … repulsive?"

"I think it might work if we were in the right mood. A nice meal, some wine, a romantic movie. Or a dirty one." He grinned, and she put her arms around him.

"So you don't want to give up?" she asked.

"We always knew it wasn't likely to work the first time. This way it might even be fun!"

"Idiot!"

"And you're forgetting that gay men probably know more about straight sex that they do about gay sex. We're bombarded by the stuff. It's in books, at the cinema, in magazines. Then when you turn on the television, there it is again. You can't get away from it. I expect I know more about women's erogenous zones than I do about my own!"

"Thanks, John." Serious now.

"I don't know why you're thanking me. It if works, I get a night of passion. You get nine months of morning sickness."

Busy writer Jay Mandal is from Southern England. After grammar school, he joined a City bank and also worked in Europe. He's written two novels and over sixty short stories – three of which have been adapted into plays – and '*Slubberdegullion*', a collection of short works. ***Speakout*** magazine published at least one Mandal story in each issue, and his short stories have been featured in popular gay publications as well as in prestigious general interest magazines, not specifically aimed at a gay readership, like ***Passport*** and ***Lookout***.

Lookout Magazine: "Written in the sympathetic, amusing and inimitable style which has become Jay's trademark. All the characters are well drawn and, in almost every one, a reader will easily identify someone they know. Jay handles dialogue extremely well and is a master of quick-witted repartee."

Neil Bartlett, Artistic Director, Lyric Theatre Hammersmith: "I read with pleasure."

Ned Sherrin, CBE, writer, director and producer: "Congratulations. I enjoyed ...."

Hanif Kureishi, writer of *My Beautiful Launderette*: "Wonderful story."

Alan Sinfield, Professor of English and American Studies, Sussex University: "Shrewd and thoughtful. I enjoyed it."

Matthew Parris, columnist, broadcaster and former MP: "Well-written: a good attention-grabbing narrative style."

Susannah York, actress and writer: "Very engaging. You characterise your people well through their speech, and sympathetically. I'd guess this would adapt well for radio, too."

A DIFFERENT KIND OF LOVE

CONTENTS

A DIFFERENT KIND OF LOVE

"Sorry."

"My fault." Clive held the door open to allow the man out. Recognising the hesitation on the part of the other, he added: "Can I help?"

"I'm not sure ..." the man said, gesturing whence he'd come.

"First time's the worst."

The other man visibly relaxed. "That obvious, is it?"

"Everyone looks shell-shocked the first time. Look, why don't you come in with me?" he suggested.

The stranger regarded Clive warily for a second, but what he saw obviously reassured him. "OK, thanks," he said, following Clive in.

"Are you gay?" demanded the man sitting at the front desk.

The stranger flinched at such directness.

"It's all right, he's with me," said Clive.

The man at the desk looked at Clive, and his face softened. "OK."

The noise, the smell, the heat hit them as soon as they went through into the club. The stranger hung back, his senses overwhelmed. Clive grinned at him, and the man smiled sheepishly back.

"Can I get you a drink?" the man asked, glancing nervously at the bar which was surrounded by a jostling throng of people.

"I'll get them," Clive said. He asked the man what he wanted, then made his way over to join the mêlée. When he glanced back, the man was watching him as if terrified that Clive would abandon him in this madhouse.

"Thanks," said the stranger when Clive returned with their drinks. "I'm Tony Clarke, by the way."

"Clive Robinson."

Tony looked around. The room was a seething mass of bodies, mostly male, some looking as if they wouldn't be out of place in a classroom. He sighed. "They all look so young."

"Most of them are."

"I feel I should have been here fifteen years ago."

"It wasn't open then."

"When I had a night out, DJs played the music – they didn't make it."

"Everything changes."

Tony glanced at him; it sounded as if he wasn't referring just to the music. Clive looked away. Tony, too, turned to survey the crowd on the floor. Men dancing with men. Eyes staring too hard.

"It can seem a bit intimidating at first," said Clive, as if reading his mind.

"Certainly unnerving."

The dancers blended together so that somehow they all looked alike.

A young man walked by, and made eye contact with Tony, who tried not to wince when he noticed that the man had a nipple-ring.

"Is it obligatory?" he asked Clive.

Clive smiled. "If you've got the nerve to have it done," he said, only half-joking.

"And that's another thing – why isn't anyone wearing a shirt? I can see only one." He paused and looked again. It was a girl. "At least her hair is nearly as long as mine."

"Fashion. It was different when I was last on the scene."

Again there was a veiled reference to something, but Tony was unsure whether to ask. He felt that Clive, despite his obvious friendliness, was quite a reserved person underneath. They lapsed into silence for a while.

"I've never seen anything like it," Tony exclaimed eventually, wondering if a nearby couple were really doing what he thought they were.

"You make it sound as if you never will again!" said Clive, laughing.

Tony smiled. "I scarcely know what to say. The word 'awful' springs to mind. And I'm not sure how I mean that."

"People do come for the dancing," Clive reassured him. "It's not just a meat market. Why did you come?"

"I suppose I needed to find out what it was like. Satisfy my curiosity. I thought maybe ..." Maybe he'd meet someone. Some chance! "D'you know a lot of the people here?" he asked.

"Quite a few. The older ones, at any rate. But there are quite a lot of new faces, or at least people who started coming when …" He broke off abruptly, his expression unreadable. "I didn't come for a while."

Suddenly blocks of light were switched on, flooding the room with a mixture of warm and cool tones, making skin glow or shine eerily green. Tony watched as a dancer stripped down to a thong. Onlookers applauded as he thrust himself towards them.

Tony tried to analyse his reactions as he watched, hypnotised. Was this freedom or licence? Was he attracted or repelled? And was this what he had come looking for?

He shook his head. "I just don't know if I'm ready for all this. I don't know if I'll ever be ready."

"Perhaps this isn't the right place for you. Not everyone can take the scene." Clive sounded matter-of-fact about it.

"It's funny – I thought I was broad-minded," Tony said ruefully. He sipped his drink, wondering if it had been such a good idea to come here. Too much, too soon. Was he just out of touch, or now, at the age of thirty-eight, simply too old for this sort of thing? If the latter, where should he had gone instead? He downed the last of his pint.

Oh, God, now his bladder was full! If this was what went on openly on the dance floor, what on earth happened in the toilets?

"Over there," said Clive.

"But that's the ladies room," objected Tony, in a horrified voice.

"Not tonight." Clive smiled, a genuine smile that reached his eyes. Tony hadn't appreciated until that moment how strained Clive had looked earlier.

Luckily the toilets were empty when Tony went in. He relieved himself as quickly as possible, then washed his hands. He was just congratulating himself that he'd emerge unscathed from the experience when the door opened, admitting two statuesque, glamorous females. Christ! Clive must have got it wrong after all!

"Sorry," he mumbled automatically. "I'm just going."

One of the women smiled. "No need to hurry," came a husky voice.

"All right?" asked Clive.

Tony nodded dumbly.

"Look, d'you want to go somewhere else?"

Startled, Tony croaked: "What?"

"A pizza or something."

Tony breathed again. "OK."

"Only it's not really your sort of thing, is it?"

"No," Tony agreed fervently. "Yeah, a pizza would be nice."

Gradually, over the meal, they found out about each other. Clive was an architect, while Tony was a partner in a small printing firm. Eventually the subject came round again to Tony's presence at the club.

"So what really brought you to Alexander's?"

"A taxi," Tony quickly retorted, and they both laughed. Then the story came out. "I was married, but things just didn't work out. Not that I was unfaithful – with anyone," he added. "Luckily there were no children, and now I'm divorced." He glanced down at his wineglass. "And I'd always wondered ..." He looked up again. "I don't know what I am. Maybe I'm just curious. Maybe tonight was it. I s'pose I might be bisexual, maybe even gay, although after all this time perhaps that's unlikely. It wasn't an unhappy marriage, we parted amicably enough. That was the trouble – we really were *just* good friends. I think my wife realised that wasn't enough, not if we were planning on having children. It was strange; on the one hand, I felt that I'd failed, but on the other, there was an enormous sense of relief. If it had been left to me, we'd still be married, still be jogging along. And I'd still be wondering. But I'm not sure what to do. And tonight ..."

"Did we scare you off?"

"You certainly opened my eyes!"

"You could try somewhere else. Maybe a club that runs a mixed night," Clive suggested.

"A mixed night?" repeated Tony, baffled.

"Gay and straight."

Tony grinned. "I wouldn't know where to start!"

The waitress returned with their credit cards.

As they stood, putting on their coats, Clive said: "Well, nice meeting you."

The words had a final ring to them.

"Look," began Tony awkwardly, "d'you think I could see you again? It's just ... there's no one else I can talk to," he added desperately.

Clive's heart sank. He didn't need this. He really didn't need this. "OK," he said at last, certain he was going to regret his decision.

"Maybe we could go to the cinema," Tony said eagerly.

"They won't thank us, not if we talk over the soundtrack."

"No, I suppose not. Another meal, then? I'll pay." He looked beseechingly at Clive.

Clive nodded. "But I'll pay for myself."

"Fine. How about next Friday? Unless you're doing something," he added diffidently.

"No, I'm not doing anything," Clive replied. His voice sounded strangely empty.

"I'm imposing. I'm sorry. We'll leave it." Tony turned away. He knew he'd asked too much, pushed too hard, intruded into someone else's life.

"Tony?" Clive had followed him out of the restaurant.

Tony stopped and looked around.

"Make it Chinese," said Clive. "You do like Chinese?"

Tony nodded, his eyes lighting up.

"The Dragon at eight o'clock, Friday. See you then."

"See you then. And Clive?"

"Yes?"

"Thanks. You didn't have to."

"Maybe ..." Clive stopped. Maybe he did? "Friday," he repeated firmly, then turned and walked quickly away.

"Of course, people think it's just about sex, but it's not, not really. I can't say I'm not curious, of course I am, but it's whether I can live with someone for the next twenty or thirty years. And, at the moment, I just don't know. For a while, I could see myself getting married again and still wondering if it was right for me. And yet the club ... It felt like I'd been thrown in at the deep end when all I wanted to do was test the water." He passed a dish of bean sprouts to Clive. "Have you always been certain you were gay?" he asked, lowering his voice.

Clive smiled. "Feels like forever," he admitted. "I certainly knew by my teens."

"There's so much I don't know," said Tony.

"Ask away," said Clive quietly.

And so Tony had asked his questions; and Clive had answered honestly. But, in spite of this, Tony was aware that Clive's answers were somehow impersonal. By the end of the meal, Tony realised that Clive had volunteered very little about his own life. He, Tony, had talked about his marriage which had lasted for over ten years, but he had no idea what Clive had been doing during all that time, and he knew Clive had deliberately evaded the subject.

Of course eventually he found out what had happened; Andrew, Clive's partner, had died from AIDS.

"So that's why ..." He broke off awkwardly.

"Why they all handle me with kid gloves?" Clive smiled gently. "Yes. That's why."

A bitter irony: Tony and his wife had been in a comfortable yet passionless marriage which both had survived; while Clive and his partner had been in a deeply loving but ultimately doomed relationship.

Christ! He looked at Clive in dread.

"It's not like cancer," said Clive, knowing what Tony was thinking. "There's always another question hovering." He smiled forlornly. "It's all right. I'm all right. We were always careful."

But what had been the point in being careful? Sometimes he thought he would welcome an end to it all.

"I'm so sorry," Tony whispered.

"Yes."

All the questions. How old was Andrew? Did his parents know he was HIV-positive? Did they even know he was gay? Had they known about Clive? Was Andrew ill for a long time? Was Clive with him?

Tony couldn't ask. Their acquaintanceship was too new, Andrew's death too recent for him to intrude. And yet ... maybe they could be good for each other if things were kept light. A simple friendship. No complications. Clive was Tony's passport to the gay community, while Tony could help Clive re-join the outside world.

"Another cup of coffee?" asked Clive, and Tony knew the subject was closed.

"We'd be practically touching knees," said Tony.

Clive smiled. "That would never do," he agreed solemnly.

"Once I move, it'll be all right." In a couple of weeks Tony would be in his new flat, but for now he occupied a bed-sit. When they separated, his wife had remained in the marital home, but that had now been sold. "Come on," he said to Clive. "The Café Noir will still be open. We can go there."

"No. Come back to my place for a cup of coffee. I don't mind."

Tony knew of Clive's reluctance to have visitors. "Look, I understand. Besides, you hardly know me. Let's go to The Café Noir."

Clive could be stubborn. "No. Maybe it's time. Maybe it's easier if we don't know each other very well. Don't worry – it's not some sort of shrine."

The house was ordinary. It was the photo that made him want to cry. A picture of Andrew and Clive, the latter looking much younger. And happier.

"Eight years ago."

Tony jumped guiltily.

"I've aged. I know I have."

"How long were you together?"

"Nearly fourteen years. We found out six years ago. And then nothing much happened for ages." Except lying to each other, pretending everything was the same. Apart from sex. They'd both been terrified of making love. What if? haunted their nights. A barrier had come between them. Clive couldn't share what Andrew was going through, couldn't tell him he understood, couldn't even hold him without the spectre of death between them. And he was forever guilty, guilty that he was the one destined to live.

They'd talked about miracle cures, but somehow they never really believed. Andrew learned acceptance. It was Clive who wanted to scream and hit out. Clive who wanted to deny the fate that had befallen them. Clive who cried when Andrew wasn't there to see.

And, since Andrew's death, this awful nothingness.

Somehow it was easier being with someone who hadn't known Andrew, who wouldn't remind Clive of something they'd done, some place they'd been. Wouldn't remind Clive that, once, life had been more than just a struggle to get through each day. The past had hurt, but he'd been alive, he'd felt things. He knew he should cry, knew he should shout and scream and howl, but there was nothing left. He was a shell, empty inside, drained dry. Andrew had died. It was over. Everything was over.

It was odd that he didn't mind being with Tony. He listened to Tony as he talked about his marriage, as Tony tried to work out what had gone wrong. Jane had reverted to her maiden name, but was still teaching at the same school. They bumped into each other, he and his ex-wife; parties to which both had been invited, Sainsbury's, that sort of thing. Tony thought his wife had been relieved, too, that they'd divorced. There were no regrets on his part. Oh, a failed marriage was nothing to boast about, but he had no wish for reconciliation. And what of the future? That was unclear, but, on the whole, he was optimistic. Clive was a great help.

Clive looked surprised. "I haven't done anything," he objected.

"You've listened," said Tony. "I really don't know anyone else that would have done as much. And you've never condemned me."

"Why should I?"

"Oh, for not knowing my own mind. For not being sure about my sexuality. You've never pushed me. You've given me plenty of time. You know," he went on with a grin, "my friends keep trying to fix me up with women."

"Does that mean I should be trying to fix you up with a man?" joked Clive.

They laughed. "I'm not sure I'm ready for that. There are so many things to consider. Could I fall in love with another man?" Tony paused for a minute. "Yes, on balance, I think I could. There's the hurdle of sex. I won't deny that it scares the living daylights out of me. But I suppose it did when I was nineteen!" Then he became serious once more. "And just being gay or bisexual – I don't know that I've got the courage. I just don't know that I could stand up and be counted. It seems so much easier being straight."

"I never had the choice," said Clive simply.

So they were company for each other. Sometimes they'd go out for a meal or to the cinema or occasionally the theatre, but just as often they'd stay in and watch television or a video. Maybe they'd get a take-away.

On this particular Saturday, they were watching a video. Clive had had a particularly bad week. Tony's presence was like balm to his soul. Then the tape finished, and Clive realised he'd got to get through another week of doing things that had lost their meaning, having to see people he'd rather avoid, acting normally when he felt so empty.

He kissed Tony. Not gently. His tongue pushed against Tony's teeth, probed Tony's mouth. He tried to bite Tony's lips, as if by hurting someone else the hurt inside him would diminish.

Tony, after his initial surprise, waited for the storm to pass. He knew it was more desperation than desire on the part of Clive.

Eventually Clive slumped back on the sofa. "Sorry," he whispered, his eyes going automatically to the photo on the cabinet.

Tony wasn't sure if Clive was apologising to him or to Andrew.

Clive felt exhausted. It wasn't really Tony he wanted. It was too soon. It was all too soon ...

"Look, you'd better go," he said to Tony.

"I'm not going anywhere while you're like this," Tony replied firmly.

"Like what?" Clive demanded truculently.

Tony said nothing.

"So you think I'm behaving oddly?" Clive said in a deceptively quiet voice. "Don't you think that half the time I just want to curl up and go to sleep so I can forget everything? Don't you understand that every morning when I wake up and find I'm still alone I could weep? I hurt and I want to lash out and hurt everyone else. And that includes you." He stared defiantly at Tony.

"What d'you want me to do?" said Tony evenly.

"Just sod off and leave me alone!" Clive yelled.

"That's much better!" said Tony approvingly.

They looked at each other, then Clive smiled. "Sod you!" he said.

"Maybe one day," Tony said mischievously.

"I hate bisexuals. You're all so indecisive."

"Best of both worlds!"

"Thanks." Serious now.

"What are friends for?" Tony said lightly.

And they both realised, with some surprise, that that's what they'd become.

For a while, Clive was all right, but then it all caught up with him again when they'd gone Christmas shopping one mild day in late November. As they sat on a bench by the river in the pleasant sunshine, he found himself crying. Hell, why now? he thought, the tears running unchecked down his face.

Tony had been rummaging in a bag for something he'd bought and wanted Clive's opinion on, when he realised Clive was very quiet. He looked up. "Christ, what's wrong?" he asked in dismay.

Clive just shook his head, unable to speak. He stood up and cast around for some way of escape but there were people everywhere so he just stood there, locked in his own private grief.

"D'you want me to go?" asked Tony helplessly. He'd stood up, too, and now was close to Clive, shielding him from inquisitive eyes.

"I want you to hold me." The words, wrung out of him at last, seemed to stem the flow of tears. He smiled shakily. "I know it's not possible. Here. Now." He blinked once or twice, then moved away from the bench and towards the river, where he leant on the parapet. He blew his nose and wiped his eyes.

Tony waited.

Finally Clive turned round. He looked calmer. "Come on," he said, "let's do some serious shopping!"

"My wife liked shopping," Tony remarked later that same day. It was a simple statement; there was no hidden criticism or implied comparison intended. He often spoke about Jane, always with affection. If only Clive would talk about Andrew. Maybe he needed prompting.

"If you want to talk ..." ventured Tony.

"I'm not sure I'm ready."

They both grinned; that was what Tony usually said about gay sex.

"You wouldn't do anything stupid, though?" Tony pursued.

Was it stupid, wanting to stop the hurt? To put an end to the numbness, to the loneliness? He saw Tony was watching him closely. "No, I won't do anything stupid. Who'd wrap all these blasted Christmas presents if I did?"

Spring gave way to summer, although the weather remained cool at night.

"I suppose if I suggested going to bed you'd run a mile?" Clive said one evening halfway through a television programme neither of them was really watching.

"It's not that far to your bedroom, is it?" joked Tony. "Are you serious?"

"Only if you want me to be. There's no pressure."

"I suppose it's what I've been wanting to find out," said Tony slowly.

"It's just ... I miss not having someone there. As they say in all those so-called adult ads, limits respected. We'd do only what you're happy with. In fact, we needn't do anything at all – I'm sure I could find you a pair of pyjamas."

"Come on," said Tony, standing up. "And you can forget the pyjamas."

They undressed, each in his own space. There was a politeness to it, an experimental, almost clinical, atmosphere.

"Sorry it's a bit chilly in here. I wasn't planning any of this," said Clive.

When he came back from the bathroom, he was checking the date on the condoms.

They'd been moving inexorably towards this for some time, perhaps ever since that day they went shopping and Clive had wept as they sat by the river.

"Look, I've really no idea what I'm doing," Tony admitted. They were both naked.

"Don't worry. I think I still remember." Clive grinned at him as he rearranged pillows.

Clive leant forward, then, very gently, began kissing Tony's mouth. Tony responded slowly at first, then with more passion as Clive's hand did its work.

Tony found himself relaxing as their two bodies became warmer. His face began to flush, his pupils dilate. He was aware that Clive was becoming aroused, too, his breathing rapid, his kisses more insistent. He could smell Clive's sweat and this triggered a response in him, his actions grew automatic, his senses were overpowering him, he was losing himself.

And, as he climaxed, what little conscious thought he had told him that he might have found what he'd been searching for.

They lay side by side. Kissed gently. Clive guided Tony's hand down.

"I thought …"

"Don't want to scare the living daylights out of you just yet!" teased Clive.

"So what did you think?" asked Clive lightly.

"I wouldn't mind doing it again," answered Tony in the same tone.

"Let me have a rest first!"

"No, I meant …" Tony suddenly realised his leg was being pulled. "What about you?"

"You were very gentle."

"Was that wrong?" asked Tony anxiously.

"No. It was nice." He kissed Tony lightly, then nuzzled the hair on his chest. "I like hairy men," he added. "And, no, Andrew wasn't hairy."

"You've been very patient."

"So have you," said Clive quietly.

"That's different. My situation was relatively simple. You've had many more emotions to deal with than I have."

"Are you staying?" asked Clive, nudging the conversation away from such a personal matter.

"If you'd like me to."

Clive smiled mischievously. "Well, it is your turn to do the washing-up," he said.

And so Tony took to staying on Friday nights and shopping with Clive on Saturdays. And, gradually, Clive started to talk about Andrew.

Another Christmas was almost upon them.

Clive found to his amazement that he wasn't dreading this one. There were parties to go to, friends to see, relatives dropping round. Even Christmas shopping had been painless, and he'd spent an enjoyable afternoon writing out Christmas cards. Tony helped him decorate the tree, once they'd got it down from the loft without any major damage being sustained either to themselves or the house; even the lights had worked first time.

They'd taken Clive's two nieces to see Father Christmas after Clive's sister had begged them to get the children out of the house so she could have five minutes' peace. She'd thought Clive and Tony would be taking them to the park, and was pleasantly surprised when, nearly three hours later, they all trooped in, tired but happy, the girls showing her the presents Santa Claus had given them. She glanced at her brother, and thought how much better he looked nowadays. Tony was obviously good for him.

Spring came.

"We need to talk," said Tony. It was ten o'clock on a Friday night. They'd been sitting in bed, reading.

Clive knew he shouldn't have been surprised. Theirs was a relationship they'd slipped into. There'd been no real effort or conscious choice on the part of either. It had been convenient for both of them to have someone to talk to, someone to go out with, someone to sleep with. For Tony, it had been a testing ground, a safe place to work out his sexuality. It was understandable that he wanted to spread his wings. And now he obviously felt it was time to move on.

And Clive – how did he feel? Empty, he had to admit. But nothing could ever be as bad as when Andrew died and he was left alone and vulnerable. He'd survive. He'd miss Tony, of course he would. Tony had understood about Andrew, had listened when Clive talked about him, had held him when he cried. Over the months, they'd grown close.

"We've always got on, haven't we?" asked Tony.

Clive wondered if he'd met someone. He smiled. "Yes. Even when you were straight." He'd make it as easy as he could for Tony. He didn't want him to feel guilty.

"It's just that I feel ready for something less casual. No, not casual – that's the wrong word. Less ..." Tony searched in vain for something better.

"More permanent. More committed," Clive suggested.

"Yes," said Tony gratefully. "It started for all the wrong reasons. You were lonely and I wanted to find out about myself. I think we're both past that stage now." He glanced at Clive to see how he was taking it.

Clive knew Tony was right; their relationship had run its course. "Go on," he said encouragingly.

"But I'd grown lazy. It was too easy just to leave things as they were rather than go off and look elsewhere. I thought inertia had set in. After all, that's what happened when I was married." He stopped again, and looked at Clive.

"We'd got used to each other. I liked being with you. Then it suddenly dawned on me that it wasn't inertia on my part – I didn't actually want to be with anyone else. It felt right being with you." He was aware that Clive wanted to say something, but he rushed on.

"I know how much you still miss Andrew, and I don't expect you to feel what you felt for him. I don't expect any promises, but I need to know if you think you can put up with me for a bit longer. You know, twenty or thirty years," he added, managing to make a joke of it, even though he was quite serious. "You see, I think I've fallen in love with you. And I'm making a complete fool of myself." He turned away, tears stinging his eyes.

Clive sat there, stunned. The 'Dear John' talk had turned into a declaration of love. He wasn't sure quite how he felt about it. But then, as Tony groped for a handkerchief, their eyes met, and Clive acknowledged at last that what he felt for Tony was love. Not the love he'd felt for Andrew, that was gone forever, but a gentle, steadfast love.

"Twenty or thirty years?" Clive repeated thoughtfully.

Tony nodded.

"Well, I don't suppose I'd ever find anyone else who actually likes cleaning the oven," Clive said gently.

Tony smiled shakily. "Jane thought I was mad, too. You think it might work, then?"

"I think we should give it a go. Mind you, I'm not looking forward to telling my sister. She'll only say 'I told you so!' "

"At least she's only your sister – I've got an ex-wife to tell!"

"Ah," said Clive.

"What d'you mean?" Tony asked suspiciously.

Clive sighed. "I was hoping I wouldn't have to mention it. The kids did a family tree at school."

"And?"

"They put me on it." He paused and looked at Tony. "And you."

"Well, I suppose it could be worse. But I still don't understand …"

"Their teacher wrote, 'Such an enlightened and enlightening effort deserves full marks. Well done!' I didn't make the connection at first. You always call your ex-wife by her first name. I knew she was a teacher, of course. Then when the kids said her name hadn't always been Jarvis ..."

"Oh, my God," said Tony. "Jane!"

For a while, they just looked at each other. Then Tony shrugged.

"Oh, well," he remarked philosophically, "I suppose that's one less person I need tell."

****

HEAD OVER HEELS

The day was clear and bright with just a hint of a breeze – perfect weather for their visit to the theme park.

There were about ten of them. Craig and Ashley, of course. Craig was tall, outgoing and a born optimist. He came up with improbably wild schemes that surprised everyone by somehow managing to work. People liked him; he made them laugh. Most of the girls had been smitten at one time or the other, but, though Craig had been friendly, none of them had succeeded in pinning him down. Then Ashley had materialised, and it became obvious why Craig had been able to resist their feminine charms. Ashley was short, quiet and sensitive. And male. And Craig was crazy about him.

Craig worked for a television company. He'd been doing some research into English poets when he'd met Ashley who worked on the information desk in the county library. Craig had found this shy young man so helpful and refreshingly knowledgeable that he'd offered to take him to lunch. In the end, they'd shared Ashley's sandwiches on a bench in the nearby gardens, and Craig had fallen head over heels in love.

They'd collected maps at the entrance and were now planning their route. First, the popular rides – the ones that plummeted and rocked and twisted and rotated at speed and sometimes in utter darkness, rides designed to terrify even the stout-hearted. They'd save the others till after lunch.

"Guard this with your life!" instructed Craig.

"Why?" asked Ashley suspiciously. "What is it?"

"Oh ... only my camera."

"All right. Do you want me to take a photo of you while you're on the Rocky Rapids?"

"No! Don't do that. I'll take some of you later."

Ashley was puzzled but didn't ask for an explanation.

"You're a girl," said Ashley. He and Jill were standing by the rails enclosing the Log Flume.

"I didn't think you were interested." She watched idly as yet another 'log' was cranked up a steep incline, teetered tantalisingly at the top, and then plunged, to the accompaniment of screams, past horizontal sprays of water into a pool which deepened just when everyone thought they were home and dry.

"I'm not. I mean not in that way. You don't like white knuckle rides, do you?"

"Is that a sexist remark?"

"Oh, you don't, do you?" Ashley's face fell.

"Well, no, as it happens." Odd, then, that her secret ambition, which she had confided to Ashley, was to learn to fly. Maybe it was the fact that up there she'd be in control.

"Will you come on the children's rides with me?" Ash begged, the idea of miniature fire engines and stage coaches beckoning appealingly.

"Where's Craig?"

"He's abandoned me. He left his stuff with me and went off with the others. I've got Martin's video camera, too. I don't know why he brought it – he's not used it yet as far as I know. Wait till they come off and then we'll give everything back and go off ourselves."

So Ashley had returned coats and cameras to their owners, and he and Jill had headed for the Children's Zone. Ashley's spirits soared as he took in the model boats on the little pond, the scaled-down racing cars zooming around an oval circuit, the tea cups spinning around a tall teapot. This was more like it! Here you could eat your candy floss or doughnut or ice cream without having to weigh the consequences.

"We're at least ten years older than anyone else on this ride. I hate looking conspicuous," said Ashley, as they cruised slowly in a Pink Elephant at an altitude of eight feet.

"I'd have thought you were used to it, hanging around with Craig!" She wondered if Ashley thought this would temporarily assuage her appetite to conquer the skies.

"We should have brought my nephew with us."

"Would he have enjoyed it?"

"Probably not. I expect it'd be too tame for him. He was fine on the Flying Fish last year. It was me that had to sit down afterwards. I pretended I'd got a stone in my shoe."

"Won't you just tell me, for heaven's sake!" said Martin, exasperated now. He'd known Craig for years – ever since primary school, in fact – and had, given Craig's popularity, begun to wonder why Craig never seemed particularly keen on any of the girls they knew. At least, now that Craig had nailed his colours to the mast, it put him in with a chance. With the girls, that is.

"No," repeated Craig, adamant.

"I ought to check it's working at least," Martin added, in an innocent voice.

Craig looked thoughtful. "OK. You can check that it's working," he conceded at last.

It was perhaps unfortunate that, just as Martin panned around, he caught someone coming out of the gents still yanking up his zip. Martin backed away hastily, straight on to Craig's foot, and gave an apologetic shrug at the stranger who was now glaring balefully at them.

"I'll ... er ... edit out that bit," Martin mumbled sheepishly. "This camcorder's not light," he complained a minute later.

"Oh, for goodness' sake, give the thing here." Craig gave an exaggerated sigh as he took possession of the camera.

"Don't drop it," instructed Martin. "Or get it wet."

Craig looked at him suspiciously.

Martin shuffled uncomfortably. "It's my Dad's," he admitted after a moment. "But what on earth do you want me to do? We've been here ages and nothing's happened."

"You're our cameraman when we go on The Swans."

"The Swans? But that's a family ride. Parents take their children on it. There's no screaming. The thrill factor is zero."

"That's the one."

"You're not going to push anyone in?" Martin asked anxiously, knowing he would be the prime candidate.

"Don't worry, I need you to work the video camera."

"Oh." Relief flooded through Martin. Then another thought struck him. "You're not going to jump in, are you?"

"Oh, no, nothing like that." Suddenly Craig relented. Why shouldn't he let Martin in on it? He explained his plan.

"So you see," he finished triumphantly, "I want this to be a day to remember."

"Well, it's the perfect setting," Martin conceded. Even the weather was on Craig's side.

"Trust me. What could possibly go wrong?"

Martin's heart sank. He knew what that meant. He'd heard it too often in the past. Craig may have been his best friend – well, since Ashley had come on the scene maybe that wasn't strictly true – but that didn't make him blind to Craig's faults. One of which was a touching faith that everything would be all right. It was a quality that was both endearing and exasperating at the same time.

"Are you going to stand there all day? This thing weighs a ton," Craig said, transferring the camcorder strap to his other shoulder.

"So you and Craig are serious, then?" asked Jill.

"I am." Ashley stared out of the cable car at the Park beneath them. Just below was the arid Desert Zone, while, to the far right, he could make out Moon Mountain with its glittering waterfalls.

"And Craig?"

"I think so. You know Craig – he never takes anything seriously." Just thinking about Craig made Ashley smile. Those blue eyes that crinkled at the corners, the nose that wasn't quite straight, and the way, when he was with someone, of making them feel that they were special.

"Still, there must be something. None of us even knew he was gay until he brought you along."

"Yes." Ashley sighed. "He could have warned me. He sprung me on his parents, too."

"What, just took you along to meet them without telling them first?"

Ashley nodded. "Or me. I'd spent the night round at his place. I was still in my disco gear. God knows what they thought!"

"But they'd known he was gay?"

"Oh, yes. For all of a week. They took it very well, all things considered. They hardly stared at all."

"Why would they stare?"

"I had green hair at the time."

"I thought you said you hated looking conspicuous?"

"It was the day after Halloween. Believe me, where we'd been, green hair was nothing!"

At four o'clock, they were all waiting in a short queue for The Swans. Just in front of them were a mother and her young son, the latter hopping excitedly from one foot to the other.

There were about twenty boats in all. They were chained together, with a gap of several yards between each, and they were pulled gently round the lake by a winch.

The mother and son were now getting into a Swan, which was then hauled forwards to allow the following Swan to dock at the small jetty. Craig and Ashley got in the back, while Martin and Jill waited for the next boat.

It was peaceful on the lake. Tranquil. Serene. The late afternoon sun sparkled on the water and made Ashley sleepy. He let his eyes close and his mind drift. He wondered idly if Heaven was like this. He smiled. Even Craig had managed to behave himself. Suddenly, as if on cue, the Swan began to rock. Ashley opened his eyes to find that Craig was clambering into the front seat.

"What are you doing?" asked Ashley in alarm, dragged reluctantly from his daydreams.

"You'll see." Craig glanced over at Martin who nodded, then turned back to face Ashley. This was it, then. He took a deep breath.

"I need a wee!" came a small voice from the boat in front.

"I love you!" Craig proclaimed a split second later.

"Sit down!" Ashley hissed.

"Is it on?" Martin asked nobody in particular, squinting down at his video camera.

"What?" said Craig.

"Yes, it's all right, it's on."

"Are you sure they allow you to use video cameras on the rides?" Ashley asked hesitantly.

"Swan number twelve," called a voice from the bank, "are you in trouble?"

"No, we're fine," Ashley shouted back, embarrassed. "Sit down, for heaven's sake!" he said to Craig.

"Ashley, will you come live with me, and be my love?" Craig was not going to give up so easily; he'd planned this for weeks. He'd come across the line in a book, and had intended learning the whole verse, maybe even the whole poem; but he was put off by all the references to fish.

"I asked you if you needed to go," came an adult voice from the nearby boat.

"But I didn't then!"

"I'm getting all this," said Martin.

"What?" This time it was Ashley.

"I said …" Craig tried again.

"I know." Ashley cut him off.

"Here." Craig searched through his bag until he found a small box. "This is for you."

It was a simple gold ring. It was only later that Ashley noticed the engraving on the inside; A&C.

"Mum, I'm desperate!" wailed the little boy.

"Sit down!" said his mother.

"Thanks," said Ashley.

"He's standing up," the child retorted, pointing at Craig.

"It's lovely," said Ashley.

"Sit down!" his mother repeated.

"I can't wait!" the little boy said.

"I suppose that's why you didn't want me to lose your stuff. I was looking after my own ring," Ashley said wryly.

"I didn't want it to fall out. Anyway, you haven't answered my question."

"Swan number twelve, please sit down at once!" ordered the voice from the bank.

"Just a minute! Well, will you?"

"Yes, you idiot!"

Craig leant over to kiss him, promptly overbalanced, and fell forwards in an ungainly heap onto Ashley's lap.

Martin caught it all on camera. Clearly visible, just to the left, was a small arc of water which had nothing to do with the fountains and jets of the park.

****

THE LAST LAUGH

"... whether to swallow it or spit it out." There was a stunned silence.

"What?" Baz demanded. Suddenly he realised the tube train had stopped in the tunnel, and everyone was now listening to their conversation. "Toothpaste, of course. What did you think I meant?"

Conversation resumed. The train lurched off towards the next station on the Northern Line.

Baz sighed. "Honestly, some people's minds ... Just because I'm Edgware's most famous gay son – probably its only gay son, famous or otherwise – everyone latches onto everything I say and interprets it how they want." Baz looked at Keith. "Well? Say something."

"I'm not sure I agree with you."

"What, that I'm the most famous? Or that I'm its only one? Still, I suppose some of the night-time visitors to Hampstead Heath must be locals," he conceded, grinning wickedly at Keith.

Keith didn't rise to the bait; he knew Baz well enough to tell when he was trying to wind him up. "I'm afraid most people would regard you at the moment as infamous rather than famous."

"Well, they don't know the whole story," said Baz, instantly becoming serious.

"So you've come home to lick your wounds."

"You've hit the nail on the head there," said Baz quietly, his face draining of colour.

"Sorry. Tell me when we get home."

Baz just nodded, unable to speak. He turned his face away, and stared unseeingly out of the window.

"Keith?" he said after a while.

"Yes?"

"It's all right, isn't it? My staying with you?"

"Of course it is," Keith said reassuringly. "You're my brother."

"That won't stop tongues wagging," said Baz. "They'll assume you're tarred with the same brush."

"Let them. I don't mind."

"No skeletons in the cupboard since I last saw you?"

"I've been leading an exemplary life."

"You should think about taking holy orders. Have you seen Mum and Dad lately?" Baz added casually.

"I bumped into Mum in the supermarket the other day."

"How was she?"

"Fine."

"Did she ask after me?"

"We were at the checkout – everyone was in a hurry. You know how it is."

"Yeah, I know how it is."

"They'll come round eventually."

"When I stop being a filthy little pervert?"

"Dad was angry."

"But that's what he thought, what they both thought. Come on, Keith, they've had plenty of time to get used to the idea – what are they waiting for?"

"They just find it difficult to accept. They grew up in a world that expected children to get married and have children of their own. They didn't exactly welcome Lindsay with open arms once they knew we'd no immediate plans to get married."

"So what hope is there for me?"

"Give them more time. Look how they changed their mind about Lindsay."

"And this, of course, has nothing to do with the fact that Lindsay's pregnant?"

Keith sighed. "I admit it's helped, but it still goes to show that Mum and Dad can change."

"So, as long as I produce an heir, I'll stop being *persona non grata*?"

"A new baby might mean a new start for everyone."

"It's difficult. I can't get over the feeling that I'm some sort of leper, an outcast."

"It was you who left."

"Before Dad had a chance to throw me out. I've got friends, work, a whole life they don't know about. Don't want to know about. They just think I'm out having unprotected sex the whole time. Destroying the fabric of society. Trampling on family values. Why are you looking at me like that?"

His brother had forgotten how sharp Baz was. "I wasn't going to mention it. Lindsay and I agreed to ask you together."

"Ask me what?"

"It'll keep."

"You can't say nothing now. Don't worry, I'll pretend you never told me, and that it's come as a complete surprise."

"You might not like the idea."

Baz was glaring at him.

"All right, all right, I'll tell you. We were going to ask you if you'd like to be godfather."

"To the baby?"

"Well, hardly to the local Mafia."

"But I'll be its uncle, anyway. Isn't that enough?"

Keith shrugged. "This way it shows that we've chosen to involve you. You still believe, don't you?"

"Yeah, for my sins. What about Mum and Dad? Have you told them yet?"

"No. We thought we'd sound you out first."

"Of course I'll do it. It's probably the closest I'll ever get to being a father," he added wryly.

Lindsay was asleep when they arrived, but she heard them come in, and struggled to get up.

"I know, I know. Barefoot and pregnant, like some sort of cliché." She smiled happily at Baz, before hugging him. "That's the best I can do," she said, laughing. "This little monster won't let me get any closer. I hope he didn't kick you? That's his favourite trick at this time of night. So how are you?"

"Oh, you know," Baz said dismissively.

"As bad as that? Of course, we've heard some things. It sounded pretty messy."

"Well, it's over now." He didn't want to talk about it. Once he started, the flood-gates would open and he wasn't ready for that.

"You're right. It's late." There'd be plenty of time to find out later. Baz sounded more brittle than usual; Lindsay had the feeling this time it was serious. "Well, I'm going to have a cup of tea. Does anyone else want one?"

Baz glanced up at Keith, who correctly interpreted his brother's expression. "No thanks," said Keith. "I think there's some beer left in the fridge. We'll have that."

Lindsay drank her tea, and then prepared to go on up to bed. At the door, she paused. "What did he say?" she asked Keith.

The two men had ended up drunk. Baz taught Keith the whole of the alternative version of the Boyzone song, not just the 'No matter if you're gay' verse he'd sung on television.

"Of course, you'll have to smarten yourselves up if you're thinking of starting a boyband," said Lindsay the next morning, as she noisily buttered a slice of toast, her actions watched by two pairs of bleary red eyes. She looked at their pale, stubbled faces and crumpled night attire: an old pair of pyjamas in the case of Keith, and a scruffy pair of underpants in Baz's. "If this is your new image, I have to say I don't care for it much. Anyone like some orange juice?" she asked brightly.

"It's amazing how quickly they forget the morning sickness," said Keith to his brother. "You'd have thought she'd be more sympathetic when it was my turn to feel rough."

"You brought this on yourself. And the other was partly your fault, too."

Baz grinned mischievously back at her. "We get the last laugh."

"I won't be doing any laughing until at least Christmas. I'll never touch a drop again," said Keith.

"Will you be there at the birth?"

"Not if I can help it," Keith muttered under his breath.

"Of course he will," said Lindsay.

"A one-off, that's what I thought it was." Baz had known that, eventually, he'd tell them. "Bad day at work, one drink too many." He shrugged. "And I just happened to be in the wrong place at the wrong time." He shifted his feet. "Of course, the next day he apologised, said he'd never do it again. I believed him. Had to let my agent know I couldn't do the evening show. She wanted to know why, so I said I'd walked into a door. Original, huh? Now you know why I'm so in demand. Next thing I know, my agent's hammering on the door, demanding to be let in so she can see for herself that I'm all right. She said ... well, that Malcolm's friends walked into a lot of doors. Even then I still believed Malcolm was telling me the truth."

Lindsay and Keith exchanged worried looks.

"The second time happened after a show. It had gone really well, and I was on a high. I didn't notice Malcolm wasn't so ecstatic until he asked me what I thought I'd been doing. He was the star of the show, not me. I suddenly realised he was jealous. I calmed down, said it was a superb show, he'd been great. But it was too late, I could see. He wasn't drunk this time. That frightened me more. I locked myself in the bathroom, but he managed to get the door open.

"He stood there. I was terrified. Then he began taking his belt off. I thought he was going to thrash me until I saw him undoing his trousers.

"Then the doorbell rang. That distracted him long enough for me to get down the stairs to the front door. It was my agent. She'd seen the show, and had come round to congratulate me. She took me back to her place, where we double-locked the doors and sat up all night, talking. She wanted me to report it, but I didn't want to. Who'd believe me, some jumped-up little nobody? They'd say I was just doing it for the publicity. They'd probably laugh – battered men don't inspire much sympathy. And, as for Malcolm, well, no one would believe it of him. He's a household name, a national institution. All he had to do was deny it. Trish kept saying, 'What if he does it again?' She thought he was bound to, there were rumours already. It just needed someone brave enough to speak up. I said I'd had enough of brave – anyway, it was my word against his." Baz shrugged. "Well, that's about it."

Lindsay broke the silence. "Keith, you've got to do something."

"Hey, this is strictly off the record," Baz said anxiously. Sometimes he forgot his brother was in the police force.

"I'll see what I can find out," Keith promised.

Trish was right; the show had been a success, so much so that Baz had been offered a regular spot on TV. He'd have been afraid that this would serve only to anger Malcolm and make him even more keen to get his revenge, but Malcolm had also received rave reviews. There were hints of a film deal in Hollywood. Despite having said that he'd never leave Britain, this time he'd apparently been made an offer he couldn't refuse, and the grapevine had it that Malcolm would soon be on his way to California.

Things seemed to have worked out all round, thought Baz, as he was preparing for the next show. Then there was a tap on the door, and Trish poked her head round.

"We've got a slight problem," she said, coming in. "A couple of guys want to see you." Someone from security followed her into the dressing room.

"They say they've got a letter for you from your brother," the man said.

Baz frowned. Why would Keith write to him at the theatre?

"I'll deal with it," said Trish, preparing to go back with the security officer.

"No," Baz said slowly. "I'll go."

He wondered if he'd done the right thing when he saw the two people waiting with another security guard. They were big, beefy men who, despite their genial smiles, oozed an indefinable sense of menace. Maybe it was this that made them look oddly alike, or, maybe they were brothers. Baz thought uncomfortably of the Krays.

"They've got tickets, sir," said the security officer, as if there might be some doubt.

Baz would have let them in without tickets rather than argue the toss. He took the envelope, and checked the writing. After a moment's hesitation, he opened it and quickly read the note inside.

"OK, sir?"

"Yes, fine. No problem." Baz looked up at the two heavies who stood waiting placidly for his reply. "Thanks," he said to them both.

"Well, better not wish you luck, I suppose," said the first one, who was a couple of inches taller than his companion. "And, in our line of work, can't really say 'break a leg' either."

"Just our little joke," said the second.

Baz smiled weakly. "Well, I hope you enjoy the show. I'm not sure it'll be quite your thing."

"We like the Arts, don't we?" said the taller one.

"Yeah. Picasso, Rembrandt," the other agreed.

"Very eclectic tastes. Caught him reading The Telegraph the other day."

"There weren't any Mirrors left when I got there."

There was an uncomfortable silence. "Thanks for coming," Baz said at last.

"Our pleasure," said the taller.

"Yeah." They turned, and began strolling away.

Baz and the security guard looked at each other.

"I'll keep an eye on them," the guard promised.

By now the two heavies were several yards along the corridor. Baz just caught the following exchange before he went back to his dressing room.

"I hear Los Angeles is very pleasant at this time of year."

"Yeah, very pleasant. Very pleasant indeed."

****

OPERATION LONELY HEART

Sam didn't know why he was reading the Lonely Hearts column in the local paper. Well, he did, in a way. He always found it a relief to know that there were so many people out there who were in the same boat. People without partners. Not that he seriously considered answering any of the ads, even the ones from people who sounded nice. Genuine, honest, reliable, GSOH, gentle, sincere, easy-going. There was always the niggling doubt at the back of his mind as to why such nice people couldn't find someone.

So why was Sam on his own? He was honest and dependable and looked OK (light blue eyes, brown hair that fell forwards despite his brushing it back, average height). But he was shy. He would gaze longingly at copies of Gay Times on display in the newsagent's and wonder if they held the key. Sometimes he'd see a nice-looking person at a party – his friends would drag him along – and he'd imagine going up to him and saying something, but usually he just sat quietly and watched. Being gay wasn't a problem because his friends – all straight – didn't know. He had the feeling they wouldn't really mind, anyway. They were united in trying to get him 'out of his shell' as they put it. Not that he just vegetated at home; he had lots of interests and did join in. But he was a follower, a listener. He got overlooked.

He glanced again at the ads. Was n/s non-smoker or non-scene? Was 'enjoys TV' as innocent as it sounded, or did it imply the advertiser was into cross-dressing? Did 'can't accommodate' mean they lived at home or was there a partner in the background?

He sighed and looked at his watch. Was that the time? He'd better get back to work.

It was Saturday before he got to the newsagent's. Hiding behind a display of mother-and-baby magazines, he stole a glance at the lifestyle titles. There it was; this month's issue of Gay Times. He tried to read the words on the cover. The picture was of Stephen Gately. Sam was sympathetic; he thought he knew how the Boyzone star must feel on coming out. Then again, any announcement he made was hardly likely to be front page news. He wondered whether there was an interview inside. Well, he supposed he'd never find out.

Suddenly he became aware of the furtive behaviour of another customer. He was edging away from the computer magazines towards the lifestyle section. Once there, he looked up and down the aisle a couple of times, then hastily grabbed something from the top shelf. From the display on which Sam's eyes had been riveted.

What happened next was to prove a source of amazement to Sam for the rest of his life. The man, on hearing voices, panicked and dropped the copy he was holding as three yobs pushed through the doors leading from the street. Rooted to the spot, the man could do nothing but watch in horror as they approached. Sam acted instinctively. He raced round the homes-and-gardens section, snatched a pc magazine from the rack and flung it on top of the copy of Gay Times, then, just to be on the safe side, he picked both up. Finally he headed for a quiet till at the back of the shop, where the female assistant, without his having to ask, slipped the two items into a bag.

The yobs never noticed a thing.

Outside the shop, Sam found himself trembling and had to sit down for a minute. He realised that was probably the bravest thing he'd ever done.

What now? he thought. He looked at the bag. It seemed flimsy. Luckily, the front of Gay Times was facing the middle, next to the computer magazine, so its title wasn't visible through the thin green plastic. Home, he decided. He hadn't finished his shopping, but that could wait. At the moment he felt as if a great big sign hung over his head announcing his purchases to the world. Besides, he was desperate to see what a gay magazine was really like. Would he be shocked? After all, even the section in the free local newspaper scandalised him. 'Limits respected' – was he normal or just inhibited or a downright prude? 'Tactile' – what did that really mean? And 'clean' – it didn't bear thinking about.

When he got home, he found only his Dad there; his Mum was out shopping.

"I'm just going up to my room," he announced, thinking that he didn't usually keep his parents so well informed as to his itinerary.

His Dad nodded, seemingly oblivious to the bag Sam was trying to hold in as natural a manner as possible. "Shall I bring you up a cup of tea in a minute?"

"No! Give me a shout, and I'll come down."

There was no lock on the door. Sam wondered whether he should take his spoils into the bathroom. He settled for removing the duvet from the bed and blocking the door with it. Then he tipped out the contents of the green bag. For a minute, he just looked at the gay magazine in awe. Then he ran a finger over the cover. It was his. He suddenly found his mouth dry and his heart pounding. He opened the magazine ...

"Sam!"

"What?" Hastily he closed the magazine, rammed it back in its bag, and stuffed the bag under his pillow.

"Tea up!" called his Dad.

Over the next week, he kept sneaking upstairs to look at his copy of Gay Times. He told his parents he was thinking of getting a new computer and was trying to make up his mind which to buy. Time and again he found himself drawn to the Lonely Hearts section. It wasn't really much different from the one in his local paper, except there the gay ads were few and far between.

In the magazine, of course, it was different: everyone was gay or at least bisexual. Sam hadn't realised there'd be so many, all searching for a one-to-one friendship or a casual relationship. Most of them sounded nice. Some even lived near, although probably not so near as those in the local paper. He didn't know how they dared buy the magazine, let alone place an ad. Perhaps they were subscribers, each month's issue discreetly delivered, maybe to the house of an understanding friend. How would he explain the arrival of an anonymous periodical to his parents? Say he'd joined some sort of club? He suddenly grinned. He supposed it was some sort of club he belonged to; but, unlike other clubs, most members went out of their way not to be recognised as such.

Then he remembered the man in the newsagent's. Sam wondered if he'd managed to buy a copy after all. Perhaps Sam would see him there again. He was certain he'd recognise him: tall, thin, curly black hair, dark eyes that had seemed enormous as the man awaited his fate. About twenty-one or -two. Sam shook his head. Too much imagination, that was his problem. He ought to do something, instead of just thinking about things. Anyway, there was no time to do anything now. He was meeting the others at three and he only just had time to change.

They did this every Saturday; went to one of the cafés which overlooked the main square. The Caffe della Piazza was light and bright and cheap, but was usually full, so they often went to the

Café de Paris opposite, with shiny black ironwork that surrounded the balcony, where they could usually get a table with a view. They could look down on the bustling crowd of shoppers and frequently spot someone they knew. In between them was the expensive Austrian Coffee House, with its delicious cream cakes. Sometimes, if it was someone's birthday, they went there. The staff in the cafés were pleasant, too, never seeming to mind how long they stayed. The Italians were cheerful, the Austrians courteous, and the French discreet.

"Look, is that Lisa? Remember Lisa? She was in her final year when we started. Always wanted to be Something In The City." Down below, a harassed-looking mum pushed a buggy containing a baby and a lot of shopping, and pulled an older child who was obviously reluctant to go anywhere.

They looked at each other and sighed. This was their fate, too. They were not Miss Brodie's crème de la crème; nor even Mr Jenkins's. Not that they'd been trouble-makers or anything; they were merely ordinary. They'd all found a job, their parents had bought them a second-hand car, and they were already saving towards a place of their own ... if they didn't blow it all on a holiday first. They were still young, after all. But Jo would never be a supermodel; Vic wouldn't ever play football for England; and Hannah would give up her idea of seeing the world. They were sensible young people.

Ten years hence, they might be married with children. (Jo, a born organiser, was already match-making). Have their own home. Be in a good job. Settled. And Sam wondered about his own life. Should he devise a ten-year plan? Step one: tell his parents he was gay. What did they know about homosexuality other than all the scare stories they read in the paper? Step two: tell his friends. They'd be intrigued. He'd be the centre of attention for weeks. He just wasn't ready. He didn't know enough himself.

"More coffee?" asked Vic.

Sam looked up. He'd scarcely touched his, and now it would be cold. He nodded, and watched as Vic and Jo, a striking girl several inches taller than Vic, went to get some more.

"Look, isn't that Gemma over there?" Hannah, always the first to notice school friends, pointed towards a table in the Caffe della Piazza opposite.

"I think you're …" Sam began, then stopped abruptly. Hannah and Gemma were waving excitedly to each other. Sam just stared. For at the table next to Gemma's sat the man he'd seen in the newsagent's.

The man, who'd been quietly drinking his coffee, looked up at the commotion from the next table, his eyes turning to see who Gemma was waving at. Recognition dawned. For a minute, he and Sam were looking at each other. Then Vic and Jo returned, and Sam lost sight of him while cups of coffee and doughnuts were handed round. When at last the other two sat down, the man from the newsagent's had gone.

Sam felt strangely disappointed.

"Who was that?" asked Jo.

Sam found himself tongue-tied.

"Oh, that was Gemma!" Hannah said airily.

Relief swept through Sam as the talk returned to their schooldays.

'Slim, dark hair, blue eyes,' he read for the umpteenth time. Most of the population fitted that description. Even he had dark hair and blue eyes; he was working on slim. The doughnuts would have to go for a start. And 'attractive' – everyone in the Lonely Hearts column was attractive. He wondered how he would describe himself. 'Nice' sounded so boring; 'quiet' sounded worse. What were his interests? Reading. Not a very sociable activity. Watching television. Scarcely adventurous. Hanging around with his old school friends. That hardly sounded mature. Still, he didn't want to attract anyone in search of good, clean adult fun, whatever that might be exactly. Then there were the bisexuals who were free during the day. Did they work nights, or did they return afterwards to a loving, unsuspecting wife?

It was all hypothetical, anyway. He'd never summon up enough courage to write in. For some reason, that reminded him of the man from the newsagent's. He'd probably thought Sam had told the others all about their little encounter. That's why he'd fled from the Caffe della Piazza.

"Have you finished with that paper?" his Mum asked.

Sam closed it quickly so she didn't see what he'd been reading.

"Anything good on TV?" she asked innocently, assuming he'd been looking at the programme guide.

"Just the usual," Sam mumbled.

He was there again the next week. They'd gone to the Café de Paris where Sam had nobly refused any cakes. He'd scanned the cafe opposite when they'd arrived, but to no avail. It was only when they were getting ready to go that he noticed the man.

"Sam!"

"What?" He dragged himself back to the present.

"I said is seven o'clock all right."

"Oh, er, yes. I'll be ready at seven," he agreed hastily.

"No, you're picking me up. It's your turn," Jo said, looking at him curiously.

"Yes, I'd forgotten. Sorry."

Jo sighed. Then she grinned. "Gemma's coming," she said, watching him closely for his reaction.

"That'll be nice."

That appeared to satisfy her.

After their evening out, Jo pleaded tiredness and asked if they could drop her off first. She'd already told Gemma about Sam's collection of tropical fish. Gemma, it appeared, was quite knowledgeable on the subject, and Sam found himself inviting her back to his parents' house. It turned out that his Mum and Gemma's often bumped into each other at the hairdresser's. He couldn't help feeling his parents looked surprised, but, nevertheless, his Mum bustled round making more tea, and his Dad turned the television off.

Even when he drove Gemma home afterwards, it was all very civilised. He'd been worried that she might have expected some sort of wrestling match, but she just hopped out of the car and said she'd see him again soon.

He had flu the next week. During his better moments, he polished off August's Gay Times, puzzling over the unusual print size and shape. Now at least he knew what it contained. He must have been depressed because, when his Mum brought him up the local paper, all the gay ads seemed to reek of double-entendre. He would be out of his depth before he started. He was making more headway with Gemma than with the man from the newsagent's. He might as well go straight.

Then he was better, and it was time for their usual Saturday afternoon spent gossiping over a coffee in the main square. Jo suggested going to the Italian café, so they walked up the steps past the neatly-manicured bay trees to the white tables with their vases of cheerful red and pink carnations. Sunlight spilled through the angled panes of the glass roof. Sam told himself not to expect too much. Sure enough, when he got there, there was no one he recognised. He ordered a cream horn, and, when it came, bit into it, heedless of any mess. Hell! he thought, grabbing a handful of paper serviettes and hurriedly wiping his mouth and chin. It was him! The other man was watching him. Not from his usual place, but from the Café de Paris opposite. Sam felt himself go red.

"Told you!" said Jo.

The others laughed good-naturedly. Sam looked wildly from one to the other. Had they guessed?

"Once I told Gemma about the fish, well, she was hooked. And of course it's the one thing Sam will talk about."

Sam gave an inward sigh of relief. They didn't know.

"So who have you got fixed up for me?" Vic enquired, joking. Everyone knew he fancied Jo and that it was mutual, although Jo hotly denied it.

"I thought Hannah."

At this, everyone except Jo burst out laughing. "If you're not going to eat that," she said loftily to Sam, "may I suggest putting it down on the plate. You're getting cream everywhere."

Sam looked down and to his dismay found that the horn had oozed blobs of cream onto his pullover and trousers. He went even redder as he caught the eye of the man opposite.

"So where are we going next?"

"Shopping!" cried Hannah gleefully.

The others gave a mock sigh. "Come on, then," said Vic, getting up.

"I think I'll give it a miss," said Sam. "I want to have another go at getting this cream off my clothes. I'll see you tonight, though."

"You're sure you don't want us to wait?" asked Jo.

"No. You go and stop Hannah blowing all her money in one afternoon." He smiled.

After they'd gone, he risked another look across the square. This time, the man didn't see him. Sam sighed, and headed for the gents to repair the damage inflicted on him by the pastry.

As he walked across the mosaic floor of the square, he was still dabbing ineffectually at the damp patch on his pullover. He bumped into someone coming the other way.

"Sorry," he said automatically.

"That's all right," came the reply.

Saturday afternoon shoppers hurried by their small oasis of stillness.

"I don't suppose …" they both said at once, stepping out of the way of an embattled mum wheeling a baby in a pushchair and struggling with a toddler and some shopping – Lisa again, Sam suddenly realised.

"Well, thank you for the other day," said the man from the newsagent's.

Sam shrugged as if it happened all the time.

"What were you going to say?" asked the man.

"Oh, nothing, really," mumbled Sam, who'd originally intended asking him if he'd like another cup of coffee, but had now lost his nerve. "You? I mean what were you going to say?"

There was a pause. Sam knew exactly how it felt.

"Their cream horns are nice, aren't they?" the man said eventually.

"Yes. But you need to concentrate and I didn't. Most of the filling fell out."

"Ah."

"What's happening?" Hannah whispered loudly from behind a pillar.

"Nothing. Absolutely nothing," said Jo through clenched teeth. Maybe their intelligence was wrong after all. Sifting fact from fiction had never been Gemma's strong point; she was too much of a romantic. And, when it came to the target, they had so little to go on. She'd already had to re-draw her battle plans when he'd popped up unexpectedly in the Café de Paris.

"I should pay you," the man said. "For the magazine," he added.

"No, that's all right. I ... er, read it. Did you want to borrow it?" Sam said, brightening visibly.

"No. That is, I bought another copy. When it was quieter."

"Oh."

"Thanks for the offer, though."

"What's going on?" Hannah hissed. She couldn't hear from where she stood.

"Shhh! They'll hear you. It seems Sam's met his match."

"What d'you mean?"

"They're both as shy as each other."

"We'll be here all day, then! I wish I'd known. I'd have worn my other shoes, these ones are killing me. I knew I should never have bought them."

"Quiet! Lisa's coming back."

The pushchair was on a collision course with the two young men. Sam dragged his companion out of the way just in time. There was no sign of recognition on Lisa's face, but the toddler's eyes lit up and he whacked Sam with his lollipop as he tried to attract his mother's attention.

"Perhaps we're in the way here," said the man from the newsagent's.

"Yes," agreed Sam.

"We could …" they both started to say.

"What?" said Sam quickly.

"Have another cup of coffee," the man suggested, his dark, mobile face looking extremely embarrassed.

"Yes!" sang Jo, punching the air triumphantly.

"What? What?" said Hannah, jumping up and down.

"Or are you meeting up with your friends again?" the man asked, giving Sam a get-out clause.

"No!" pleaded Jo. "Don't do this to me!"

"What?" said Hannah again. She waved at Vic who had just stuck his head out from behind a stall selling flowers.

"Yes. Well, later. Not now. So I could," Sam muttered incoherently, "come for a coffee." He managed a tentative smile.

There was a pause. "Well ... shall we?"

Sam nodded.

There was then a brief interlude during which Jo's blood pressure soared as she watched the pas-de-deux taking place in the main square. Sam had begun to head for the Café de Paris, while his companion went towards the Caffe della Piazza. Realising their mistake, they both reversed direction, again each heading for a different café. Then they stopped.

"You decide," said Sam.

"We could compromise."

"I don't believe it!" exclaimed Jo frustratedly.

"Tell me! Where are they going?" Hannah was now hopping from one foot to the other. "I can't wait much longer. All that coffee!"

"How?" asked Sam.

"The other café. You know, the posh one."

Sam's face fell. The Austrian Coffee House was expensive; he didn't know if he had enough money. Besides, now he was both messy and sticky.

"My treat," said the other man.

"Do I look all right?" asked Sam, still worried about his appearance.

"You look ... fine," his companion mumbled, looking anywhere but at Sam.

Sam realised it had sounded as if he'd been fishing for compliments and, inwardly, he squirmed. However, he was effectively distracted by the sight of Hannah as she raced by on course for the ladies' loo.

"OK," Sam agreed, puzzled. Was that Vic near that display of potted plants?

Passers-by wondered why the tall girl was banging her head against the pillar.

With her troops in disarray, Hannah had deserted. Vic, on seeing Hannah break cover, had assumed the mission was over and was casually drifting about in full view. And Lisa was missing in action (actually, she was changing the baby in the Mother and Baby room at Boots and had delegated the task of watching out for Sam to the toddler who was now surrounded by several anxious assistants). Jo took the one course of action left to her – she retreated.

Sam floated home in a state of euphoria. Claude, for that was his new friend's name, had asked him where he and the others were going tonight. Sam had told him, certain that Claude would be there, too. Not that it was a date or anything. Neither of them was up to arranging something so specific. Not yet, at least. Even finding his mouth still smeared with chocolate failed to dampen Sam's spirits. He was in love!

He didn't bother to put the duvet up against the door. He felt under his pillow and drew out the familiar green bag, and pulled out the magazine, expecting Stephen Gately to be staring back at him. Instead, there was a face he didn't recognize. It must be the back cover. He turned it over, then back to what was indisputably the front. It was the September issue.

Downstairs, his Mum said: “I washed the duvet cover this morning. With this nice weather, I thought it would dry quickly.”

“Right,” said Sam’s Dad.

“And I did the one in Sam’s room, and the matching pillowcase. Then I had a look round the shops.”

“Buy anything much?” Sam’s Dad enquired over his newspaper.

“No. Nothing special,” Sam’s Mum said softly. “Just the odd magazine or two.”

****

LITTLE VENICE

"You find out I'm fifteen, so you're gonna drop me, right? 'Cos I'm too young to have sex with you. But what about me? What about what I want?"

He stormed off.

"What do you want?" Gordon asked, catching him up.

Joe halted in his tracks. "Fuck you care?" he said belligerently.

"So why d'you think I'm here? Just for a bit of underage sex I could go to prison for?" Joe hadn't told him his real age, and they'd slept together before Joe knew that Gordon was a nurse on the children's ward of the local hospital. "You're right, I didn't realise you were only fifteen. But I'm not some pervert trying to lure young boys into my car for just one thing. Surely you know that by now?"

Joe's eyes softened. "All right, you're not a pervert. So sex is officially off the menu?"

"I think so, don't you?"

"You weren't the first."

Gordon sighed. "No, I didn't think I was."

"And you still want to stick around?"

"Yes, I still want to stick around."

"You'll be taking me home to meet your parents next," Joe said, beginning to regret that he'd lost his temper.

"Does that bother you?"

"Not as much as it would bother them."

"Friends?" Gordon asked.

"Yeah, I suppose so."

They continued walking along the High Street. Occasionally Joe would stop to look in a shop window at a display of hi-fis or something similar.

"What are we going to do?" he said eventually.

"Are you hungry?"

"Not really."

"What about the cinema, then?"

"Nothing on. Besides, I haven't any money."

"I could lend …"

"No. I know what we could do," Joe said, as if he'd just thought of it.

"What?"

"You'll see."

"Is this some sort of test?"

"Maybe. Are you coming?" Joe had already started walking.

"OK."

"Don't worry, it's nothing illegal. Well, not really."

Gordon followed Joe. They turned right, away from the centre. Soon the shops gave way to flats, then the flats in turn became large houses set in their own grounds. Stafford Park, known locally as Little Venice on account of the streams and bridges at its centre, was on their left.

"How much further?" Gordon asked.

"Not far now." Joe seemed excited at something.

They stopped at the park gates, which were locked for the night.

"We're here," announced Joe.

"But it's closed."

"I know a way in."

"Are you sure this is safe?"

"You're not scared of a few guys looking to score one way or another, are you?" Joe grinned. "It's OK. The drug-pushers use one end of the park, while the cruisers use the other. No one comes to this part."

"Why are we here, then?" Gordon asked, not completely reassured.

"You'll have to be patient. I can't even promise ..." He broke off. "Here. There's a gap in the hedge."

Gordon hesitated.

"It's all right, I swear."

And there was something in his voice that finally convinced Gordon.

He squeezed through the hedge, followed by Joe, who then led him deeper into the wood until they emerged in a little clearing where there was a single bench and a statue of a girl.

"I think it's meant to be a wood nymph," Joe said, as he sat down.

"It's very nice," Gordon duly responded.

"Now we just wait."

"Wait? What for?"

"You'll see. At least I hope you will."

They waited. Joe seemed content to sit quietly, but Gordon became restless. He was about to stand up, when Joe put a restraining hand on his arm. "Keep still – I can hear something."

Alarmed, Gordon turned to Joe only to find him staring intently towards the bushes to their right. Gordon looked, too, but saw nothing. Then he heard it; a quiet rustling sound that was getting nearer. Suddenly a head appeared – black with a white stripe down the middle. The animal padded out into the clearing, followed by a second, then a third, and finally a fourth, sniffing the air as they came.

"Badgers!" Gordon exclaimed softly.

Joe just smiled.

Gordon watched them as they moved about the clearing. They were stout creatures with short, black legs and stubby tails. Their large front claws combined with their strong shoulders looked ideal for digging. Bright eyes shone intelligently from an unmistakable face.

No wonder Joe had been so evasive. "How long have you been coming here?" Gordon asked.

"A couple of years, on and off. Sometimes they come out, sometimes they don't. At first, they were wary – we both were – but now I think they've decided I'm harmless. Look, that one's a female." He pointed to a largish badger.

"And the others? They're all smaller."

"They're her cubs."

They sat there, watching the animals who seemed attracted by a fallen tree trunk. Gordon wasn't sure if the mother was sharpening her claws on it or looking for beetles as she scratched at the bark. The three youngsters soon lost interest, and began to play. They paid no attention to the two humans. For this Gordon was grateful. The adult was a hefty creature with powerful jaws that, if their owner was so inclined, could easily inflict considerable damage.

"I think they raid the dustbins," Joe said quietly. "People assume it's foxes or domestic cats. But their main diet is earthworms and insects."

"D'you bring them food?"

"No. I didn't want them to get dependent on humans. Besides, I can't come every day."

"Do they stay here all night?"

"No, they usually move on. I thought about following them once, but didn't want to frighten them. Anyway, I was getting tired. Maybe one night I'll see where they go. It's not important, though. The main thing is just seeing them."

"Have you taken any photos?"

"No. I was afraid that might scare them off. And I didn't want anyone to know they were here."

"You told me."

"I owed you an apology. I thought this might do instead. I haven't told anyone about us, you know. At first I thought it was just a one-night stand – you're not my usual type. I know, I know, I don't need the lecture. Sex within the context of a stable relationship. Only no one I knew wanted a relationship, at least not with me.

"When I come here, I see how simple life can be. I start wondering how my life got so complicated."

"Am I a complication?"

"Yes. I never expected … But I've messed that up, too. Most people don't even ask how old you are, and, when you did, I lied. I thought I'd tell you afterwards, that it wouldn't make a difference. Then I found that what we'd done was too serious. It couldn't go on. I was stupid to think it could."

"Give it time," Gordon said quietly.

"Till I'm sixteen? Eighteen? I could be dead by then."

Gordon wanted to tell him he was being melodramatic, wanted to reassure him, but he knew there was an element of truth in Joe's words. Most people would have said that it was a wild crowd he mixed with – certainly a volatile one. Instead Gordon said the only thing he could think of.

"The badgers would miss you." It sounded corny even to him.

"And you? Would you miss me?"

"Yes, I'd miss you."

Joe looked at him as if to check that he was serious. What he saw seemed to satisfy him.

"They're going now."

Gordon glanced over, and found that the badgers had indeed stopped playing, and were now trotting along a well-worn path opposite where he and Joe sat. Soon they had disappeared through a gap in the bushes, and the clearing was quiet once more.

"We'll give them a few minutes to get clear, then we'll leave."

"They certainly seem used to you. How did you know they were here?" Gordon asked.

"The first time was an accident. Chance. I'd been sitting here, and was just about to go, when I heard something. I wasn't sure whether I should run – maybe I'd stumbled on something I shouldn't have. Then I saw the badger. I don't think he noticed me – they've got fairly poor eyesight, you know. They rely on their sense of smell, so I suppose I was lucky that I was downwind of him. He was pretty big – I didn't realise they were that big – and, if I'd known they can sometimes be aggressive towards humans, perhaps I wouldn't have hung around. But it was OK. So I started coming here a couple of times a week. Sometimes I'd be lucky, sometimes not. Then this year, there were the cubs. I saw them first in April – they were much smaller then, and stuck close to their mother. Now they romp around quite happily. I was worried that the sow might chase me away, but she doesn't seem to mind me being here. I hope the biology lesson hasn't bored you. It's funny – at school I hated biology."

"So did I," Gordon admitted.

"Well, don't expect any great insights on anything else. When I realised I didn't really know much about badgers, I went along to the library to look them up. There wasn't much there."

"Perhaps you should write something."

"I'm no good at stuff like that."

"How d'you know unless you try?"

"The teachers at school all said I had a short attention-span."

"If they'd been right, you wouldn't bother coming here night after night."

"It's different here. There's no one to shout at you, no one hassling you."

"I'm sorry. Now I'm the one hassling you."

"I'll let you off. Come on, we can go now." Joe got to his feet.

Gordon realised it was now completely dark. He hoped Joe knew his way back, but he needn't have worried. Joe had made this trip too many times, and had no trouble leading Gordon through the woods to the gap in the hedge.

"D'you want a lift home?" Gordon asked as they headed back to the town centre.

"No, I'll walk." Joe had never let Gordon drive him home, never even said where he lived.

"Be careful, then."

"I will."

"You'll phone me?" Gordon knew the number of Joe's mobile phone, but Joe had always preferred to be the one to get in touch.

"I'll phone you."

"Promise?"

"You don't get rid of me that easily," Joe said lightly. "Look, you'd better go."

In the distance Gordon could see a group of youths coming towards them. Amongst them was the tall kid with the spiky blond hair. Joe was right; Gordon had better leave before the group caught up with them.

"Take care," he said, then he turned and walked away.

He thought about Joe a lot. Joe saw himself as being outside society, maybe even outside the law. To him, his age was unimportant, immaterial. He'd be sixteen in a couple of months, anyway. Legal. Gordon prayed that he wouldn't say anything to the others. He had visions of blackmail threats or of being beaten up in a dark alley. They could even go to the authorities. Losing his job might be just the start; for all he knew he could end up on some sex offenders register. Gordon tried to forget his misgivings.

Joe had been thinking about things, too. He'd always vowed to himself that he wouldn't tell anyone about the badgers. The fewer people that knew, the better. So what had possessed him to show Gordon? OK, he liked the guy, but he was nothing special.

"You gonna use that spray can, or what?" Zack, the spiky-haired leader of the gang of teenagers asked.

"Yeah. I thought you could do with a new image, so I was gonna start with your hair."

They stared at each other while the others looked on in interest. Then Zack smiled lazily. "Not bad, kid, not bad."

The tension eased. Frankie glared at Joe, warning him that he, Frankie, would be watching him, showing that he wouldn't have let Joe off so lightly.

"Wanna do something?" Joe asked, his mobile phone pressed close to his ear.

"I'm on duty in a couple of hours," said Gordon.

"I'll come round, then."

"No. Let's go for a coffee."

"Keeping temptation at arm's length?"

"Something like that. D'you know The Café on the Corner?"

Joe was reading The Sunday Times when he arrived. Gordon got them both a cup of coffee. "Is something wrong?"

Joe looked up. "I've had another row with my parents. The usual thing – why don't I get a job, or at least go back to school. This time they threatened to cut off my allowance."

"What are you going to do?" Gordon asked.

"Nothing. Just wait for it to blow over. You think they're right, don't you?" he said, catching Gordon off-guard.

"They're probably worried about you."

"They never have been before."

"Perhaps they think you'll still be hanging around the streets in five years' time."

"There are worse things. Look at my parents and their friends, for instance, playing their power games with other people's money, and making a fortune for themselves while they do it."

"You don't have to be like them."

"But I am! At least that's what my father said. He was a drop-out in the late sixties and early seventies, went on all the marches – ban the bomb, US troops out of Vietnam, equal rights for everyone. Now look at him. And he says I'll be the same in a few years. That I'm only messing about now because I know when I'm eighteen I can get my hands on the money my grandmother left me.

"So you see, I'm no better than them."

"Then prove that they're wrong! Do something with the money you get. Use it to travel or to become a nurse or a doctor or a social worker if that appeals to you. Give it all to charity if that's what you want. But don't give up. Just because your parents say you'll end up like them doesn't mean you have to. It's your life. It's up to you."

"Nice pep talk. No, I mean it. So what if I am some poor little rich kid? I can still change the world."

"Is that what you'd like to do?"

"It'd be a start. Hell, that was Frankie. I wonder if he saw us."

"Frankie? Is he the tall one?"

"No, that's Zack. Frankie is his friend. If I were Zack, I'd be watching my back."

"Will he say anything?"

"Bound to, if he recognised us. He'll be wondering how I could afford to come here. Don't worry – if he asks, I'll say you're my cousin. That my father's been putting pressure on me to come home." He took a sip of his coffee. "What about you? Any news from the front?"

"A few more casualties. Oh, and I'm going on a course. Paediatric life support."

"When?"

"When there's a place available. So I might be away for a couple of weeks."

It was pure chance that Gordon had seen the police cars. He'd spent the evening with his sister and her husband, and was driving back to the nurses' home when his attention was caught by the flashing lights in the distance. Although off duty, he decided to go and see if he could help. It was only when he got closer that he realised there were no ambulances there. Just another drunken brawl, he thought, or maybe a raid to catch the drug-pushers.

Then he saw them … the bunch of youths that Joe hung around with. They were standing quietly, some distance from the police cars, looking subdued. Joe wasn't with them.

Instantly Gordon became worried. Where was Joe? Surely he hadn't been arrested or, God forbid, injured and taken to hospital? Hurriedly, Gordon pulled over and got out of the car. Only then did he notice Joe standing on his own by the park gates. They were wide open despite the late hour.

"Joe? What's happened? Are you all right?"

Joe looked up. His eyes were pools of blank horror. "The badgers," he said.

"It's all my fault," he continued dully. "I should have left them alone. I shouldn't have come here so often. Then it would have been all right."

"Of course it's not your fault," said Gordon. "You meant them no harm."

"Frankie got suspicious when I kept going off on my own and wouldn't say where I'd been. He must have followed me. That's how he found out. So you see it's all my fault."

"Frankie did this?"

"He told some people he knew. They brought along the dogs. The ones the dogs didn't kill, the men finished off with spades. By the time the police got here, it was all over."

"Did they catch them?"

"Oh, yes, they caught them."

"And Frankie?"

"He ran off when he heard the sirens."

"What are Zack and the others doing here?"

"The police rounded up everyone in the park. They'd been here spraying graffiti on the groundsman's hut."

Joe phoned once, just to say he was all right, then a week went by without any call from him. Gordon knew he had to do something, that he couldn't let Joe deal with this on his own. He tried ringing Joe, but his mobile phone was switched off. He even tracked down the telephone number of Joe's parents, but knew as soon as his mother picked up the receiver and said: "Joe? Is that you?" that they hadn't seen him either.

Joe's mother had already contacted the police, but was able to tell them very little about her son's activities. Even so, she was concerned that she'd said too much, that Joe wouldn't thank her for bringing the authorities into it. Given Joe's lifestyle, the police weren't optimistic; they thought Joe might be anywhere.

"Who's asking?"

"I'm a friend," said Gordon. "I'm worried about him."

"His father didn't send you, then?" Zack asked. His hair, still spiky, was now a vivid shade of red.

"No."

"I thought you were his cousin," someone else said.

"No, just a friend," Gordon said tiredly. Maybe asking the group of kids Joe went around with hadn't been such a good idea. He became aware of Zack's eyes on him, as if he was being assessed.

"I haven't seen him," Zack said at last. "He was around for a while, then he dropped out of sight. I don't know where he is. Frankie's disappeared, too."

There was nothing more he could do, thought Gordon. No one else to ask, nowhere left to look.

"If I see him, I'll tell him you were looking for him," Zack said.

"Thanks." Gordon had already turned when Zack spoke again.

"I'm sorry – about everything. I didn't know ..." He shrugged.

Gordon nodded, surprised at the genuine regret in Zack's voice. They stared at each other, neither of them knowing what else to say.

Gordon was away on a course for a fortnight, and missed the item in the local newspaper. The paper was full of election news, so it was on page five, a paragraph tucked away between a sponsored parachute jump which had had to be postponed and an item on the temporary closure of one of the town's minor roads.

Death in Little Venice

Last night, the body of a young man was discovered in Little Venice Park. Death appears to have been the result of a drugs overdose. The Park is a well-known haunt of pushers and gay men.

Councillor Green has called it a scandal, and has demanded police action to stamp out such activities. The Park was recently in the news when it was the scene of a vicious attack by a gang of local youths on a badger colony.

****

CUPID

Andrew felt as if he'd been standing in the icy water for hours. He'd lost his swimming trunks when a particularly strong wave had come along and taken them with it, and now he was stuck. The tide seemed to be going out, so he had to go with it – much further and he'd be in France.

"Excuse me!"

The other man stopped swimming and looked around.

"Yes?"

"I wonder if you could help. I've lost my swimming trunks."

"D'you want me to look for them?" The man had taken off his goggles, but was preparing to don them once more.

"No. They're long gone. You couldn't get my underpants, could you? I know it's asking a lot ..."

"That's all right. Where are they?"

"Well, you see that blue flag? I'm near there. Well, my things are. Between the flag and that yellow beach umbrella – there's a black bag and a beach mat. Everything's in the bag."

The man smiled. "No trouble." He had a local accent.

It was only after the man had set off that Andrew had a sudden blinding vision of what he would find in the bag: Andrew's pink underpants, emblazoned 'proud' on the front and, on the reverse, 'and gay'. He resigned himself to never seeing him again.

"Sorry it took me so long. I couldn't find your towel, so I brought mine. I thought you might need it." The man had returned after all.

Andrew smiled his thanks and gratefully put on his pink pants and wrapped the other man's towel around his waist. "I didn't bring a towel. I thought I'd just let the sun dry me. Sorry."

They walked back to where Andrew's beach mat lay.

"I had visions of being stuck out there till nightfall, but my shoulders were beginning to burn, while my nether regions were freezing. I don't know what I'd have done if you hadn't come along."

"There must have been other people."

"Oh, there were. There was a little girl who asked her mother why I didn't have any clothes on. Luckily, her mother wasn't listening. And then there were half a dozen teenagers. I just couldn't bring myself to say anything. I'm sure they'd have laughed. By the time you came along, I was desperate."

Andrew supposed he should put his trousers on, even though he was still wet. Etiquette surely forbade him from using the stranger's towel to dry himself with. He took his trousers from his bag and, still sitting on the beach mat, managed to wriggle into them without revealing the motto on his underpants.

He handed the towel back to the other man.

"Thanks. My name's Mike, by the way," said his rescuer.

"Andrew. You sound local."

"Yes. All my life. What about you?"

"I don't live far. I moved here about five years ago. I thought I'd spend the day here. On the beach, I mean, not in the water," he said ruefully. "I'd have spent even longer there if it hadn't been for you. I wasn't sure you'd come back."

Mike looked puzzled.

"When you saw what I expected you to fetch."

"I must admit I was a bit surprised. Still, each to his own ..."

"You're not ...?"

"No, I'm not."

"Pity," Andrew said before he could stop himself.

"I'll take that as a compliment," Mike said, apparently unfazed.

They grinned at each other.

"I'd better put some sun cream on, I suppose." He got a bottle out of his bag. It said 'shampoo' on the label. "I don't believe it," he said slowly.

"What?"

Andrew showed him the bottle.

"Not your day, is it?" Mike said sympathetically.

"I just grabbed the first bottle I came to. I'd forgotten I'd washed my hair yesterday." Now he'd have to wear his tee-shirt, too. He might as well pack up and go home.

"What are you doing?" asked Mike as Andrew rolled up his beach mat.

"Calling it a day. It's no use. Today just wasn't meant to be," he said dispiritedly.

"It's still early."

"I know. It's just ... everything's gone wrong."

"Can't get much worse, then, can it?"

"No, you're right. But I haven't any swimming trunks or sun cream ... There's just no point staying."

"Look, I've got my car. We'll drive into town, buy you some trunks and sun lotion. We'll be back here in an hour."

"And when we get back here, you'll have lost your parking space."

"So we'll walk."

Andrew was weakening. "But it'll take quite a long time. Why on earth should you?"

"I have my reasons," Mike said enigmatically.

"I don't understand. Especially if you're not ..."

"Gay? Let's just say that, having saved you, I now feel responsible for you." For some reason Andrew didn't fully understand, Mike's eyes were dancing mischievously.

"No!" Mike said firmly. Then he caught sight of Andrew's wistful expression and relented. "Well, it's up to you. You're going to be the one wearing it, after all."

Andrew had been admiring a thong. "I suppose it wouldn't be very comfortable."

"Or practical."

"Not for the beach," Andrew said thoughtlessly, then went scarlet. "Sorry, I keep forgetting ..."

"Don't worry. I'm not easily embarrassed."

"Maybe the blue ones. They're nice. And practical." He sighed.

"Go on, get them both, then. Have you got enough money?" Andrew had already bought a bright blue beach towel, just in case, and some sun cream.

Andrew nodded. He took both pairs to the cash desk.

"Sorry, I was ..."

"Just looking?"

On the way back, Andrew's attention had been distracted by a display of polo shirts. There was one that just matched his new trunks.

"I'll wait while you try it on."

"Are you sure?"

"I'm used to it," Mike said in a long-suffering tone.

"You've got a sister!" said Andrew triumphantly. "Or a girlfriend."

"A sister. And a brother."

"Older or younger?"

"My sister's older, my brother's younger. They both like shopping, and sometimes I get dragged round. I've got used to it."

"Look, I won't be long. I promise!"

He was as good as his word. If it hadn't been for the sunglasses, they'd have made it out of the shop.

Eventually they got back to the beach.

Andrew looked indecisively at his range of swimwear.

"I can bear it if you can!" teased Mike good-naturedly.

"Maybe the shorts," said Andrew, fingering the thong regretfully. He'd have got more of a tan wearing the thong.

"Keep the other for special occasions."

"Thanks for ... you know …" Andrew shrugged "… helping."

"Well, I needed a few more brownie points."

"I just can't get over how laid back you are."

"Comes from practice."

"Take me home!" Andrew ordered. "I'm not well. It must have been all that sun on my head when I was in the sea. I'm seeing double!"

Mike laughed.

The second Mike just smiled, which puzzled Andrew.

"It's all right," said Mike. "You're not seeing double. This is Mark, my brother."

"But you're identical!"

"He's my twin. We're fraternal twins, actually, but everyone thinks we're identical."

Andrew looked from one to the other. They certainly looked alike, even though, as he should have realised, they weren't dressed alike.

"I finished early," Mark said to Mike. "I thought I might find you here." He glanced with interest at Andrew. Introductions were made. Mark's eyes lingered on Andrew, on the shopping bags. He looked questioningly at Mike.

"Andrew did a bit of shopping," Mike explained. An unspoken message passed between them. Mark glanced back at Andrew. Suddenly Andrew realised the two brothers were different in one vital respect.

"What did you buy?" Mark asked.

"Oh, nothing much. These trunks," Andrew said, gesturing to the pair he had on. "A polo-shirt. A pair of sunglasses. And … er ... this." He opened the bag containing the thong.

"Nice," said Mark approvingly. He smiled the same smile that his brother smiled yet which, on him, held a hint of something more.

"I hope it fits. I haven't tried it on yet."

"You'll have to give me a twirl when you do. So how did you two meet?"

"Mike came to my rescue. My swimming trunks came off in the sea, and he went to get a towel. I'm sure you'd have done the same."

"Eventually," Mark agreed, tongue-in-cheek.

Andrew wondered if they told each other everything. It had been very cold in that water. "Do people get you muddled up?"

"Yes," they both said.

"Especially on the phone," said Mike. "I've had some very enlightening conversations."

Mark stripped off his shorts and tee-shirt. Andrew looked with undisguised admiration at his body, and then shrugged apologetically at Mike. Same body, but different.

"Anyway, now I'm here, I'm going for a swim. Anyone joining me?"

Andrew scrambled up.

"You could do a bit more wave-jumping," suggested Mike mischievously. That was how Andrew had lost his trunks in the first place.

"Come on!" Mark held out his hand, and, a little shyly, Andrew took it. No one seemed to notice.

"Have fun, children," Mike said, smiling. He watched them run down to the sea. Mark, who was used to the temperature of the water, ran straight in. Andrew dithered, with the result that he was pulled over and got soaked. Mike shook his head … it definitely wasn't Andrew's day. Then he realised that Andrew didn't seem to mind one bit.

****

CHILD OF LIBERTY

"Well, I suppose that's it," said the man standing next to her.

"Mmm. It always seems a bit flat afterwards," she said.

"Yes. Are you staying for the dancing?"

"I wasn't planning to. What about you?"

"I'm not fussed."

"You're not with anyone, then?"

"No. How about you?"

"No." Lindsay shivered. Now that the bride and groom had left, she was aware how cold it was outside.

"D'you want to go somewhere for a coffee?" he asked.

Startled, she looked blankly at him.

"It's still early," he added.

Despite the chill in the air and the fading light, it was only just gone eight. Music drifted out from the hotel where the reception had been held. Children still raced about, while the bridesmaids would be smoothing down their pale blue dresses, and older couples trying to waltz to the modern songs.

"We should say goodbye to Sarah's parents," Lindsay said.

"I don't really know them," said the man.

"You're a friend of the groom, then?"

"I'm his cousin. We used to play together when we were younger, but we don't see much of each other now. I noticed you sitting on the bride's side."

"Yes. I'm a friend of her sister's. I didn't really expect to be invited."

"It seems like everyone's got married now."

"Not you, though?" The question was out before she knew it. "I'm sorry. I'm being nosy."

"That's OK. No, I've never been married. A couple more years, and I'll have reached confirmed bachelor status."

"I'm not, either. Married, that is. I'm sorry – I think I've had too much to drink. I'm not usually this tactless."

Her companion grinned. "You can't have had that much or you wouldn't even be apologising."

"I suppose not. I get nervous, you see. Talk too much, say the wrong thing. Like I'm doing now."

"It doesn't bother me. What about that coffee?" he reminded her.

"I'm not sure." She didn't know him, wasn't used to being asked out.

He saw her reluctance. "You can check my bona fides with Sarah's sister. My name's John Savage."

There was a subtle change in Lindsay's expression.

John gave a rueful grin. "I see my reputation's preceded me. I hope that means you'll accept my invitation."

They ended up in a wine bar.

"I think I'll stick to coffee," Lindsay said.

"Me, too. D'you want anything to eat?"

"A sandwich would be nice. I shouldn't really," she said, when John put the baguette down in front of her. "I need to lose weight. I'm trying to cut out sugar to see if that will help."

"You're not overweight."

"Mmm. But there's not an ounce of fat on you."

"Men have a different shape, that's all. You look fine to me."

"Thanks," she said, touched.

"I suppose my opinion doesn't really count, though."

"Of course it does!" she said vehemently. "If one of the girls at work told me …" She stopped, appalled. "Everyone's opinion matters. I didn't mean to imply …"

"I do notice women. But you're right; it's probably a more detached kind of interest. Maybe that makes it more objective."

"Sometimes you don't want objective," Lindsay said, her eyes suddenly bright.

"I've upset you. I'm sorry."

"No, it's just that you were kind. I'm not usually this emotional. It's just everything – the wedding, the wine, talking to someone. Give me a minute and I'll be all right."

John took the opportunity to look around the wine bar. It was busy – well, it would be at this time on a Saturday – and the long mirrored wall reflected the chrome and glass interior, and made it look larger than it really was. At the tables people were enjoying a bottle of wine before heading elsewhere for the evening. He and some friends had done the same thing five or six years earlier. That was before they knew about him. Gradually, the group had fragmented into couples, and, one by one, the couples had got married.

He glanced up to find Lindsay watching him.

"You looked miles away," she said.

"I was. How are you feeling?"

"Fine now. D'you know where they're going for their honeymoon?"

"Venice."

"It sounds lovely."

"Yes. I liked Venice."

She wondered who he had gone with.

"I've stayed in Verona," she said. "The day we were meant to be going to Venice I came down with a stomach bug, and couldn't go. Since then I've always wanted to go back to Italy, and see what I missed."

"Maybe you'll go one day."

Again she was struck by his gentle sympathy. "Look," she said, "why don't we go out for a proper meal next week? To a restaurant, I mean. I'd like to repay you for the baguette."

"There's no need."

"And for listening."

"I've enjoyed your company."

"I don't seem to have asked you anything."

"I lead a very quiet life," he said, smiling. "Are you OK to drive? Should I get you a cab?"

"I think that would be wise. What about you?"

"Me? Oh, I'm always sober," he said lightly, but beneath it she detected a trace of loneliness.

"Let me have your phone number. I'll arrange something, and give you a ring." Suddenly she was assailed by doubts. Was she being pushy? "I'm sorry. You're probably busy."

He shook his head. "No. A meal would be nice. But we split the bill."

"They didn't want to travel too far," he was saying, "what with the baby due in a few months' time." He sensed her stillness.

"I didn't know," she said quietly.

"I think they just told the family. Here, have some water."

Her hand shook as she took the glass.

"I'm sorry I mentioned it. I didn't realise it would upset you."

"You weren't to know." Gradually the colour was returning to her cheeks.

They sat in silence. At last Lindsay spoke.

"I've got a good job, a nice house, and yet lately it's not seemed enough. If I tell you, you'll think I'm just some hysterical female, another Bridget Jones whose biological clock is ticking away." She paused. "I want a baby," she said.

"A baby?" he said in a neutral tone of voice.

"Yes, a baby. Not a designer one that I can show off to my friends at work, and dress up in overpriced baby clothes, but a real baby. One that wakes during the night, one that's sick over my dressing-gown, one that cries and cries until I end up crying, too. I'm sorry. I've never told anyone else. I must be embarrassing you."

"No, you're not. Everyone has a dream."

"Sometimes I think mine's beyond my reach. Here I am, thirty-six, spinster of this parish ... I've never even been close to getting married."

"You'll meet someone."

"Everyone thinks my career's the most important thing in my life, but that's only because there's been nothing else. I'd give it up tomorrow if I had the chance." She paused, then said: "I'm doing it again."

"Doing what?"

"All the talking. You haven't told me your dream."

"Me? Oh, I just want someone I can love."

They'd seen a lot of each other since the wedding, and were fast becoming friends. Neither was especially close to anyone of their own sex; Lindsay, because she'd been so work-orientated that her private life was virtually non-existent, and John in case friendship turned into something more on his part.

That evening they'd been to the cinema, and had decided to go back to Lindsay's house to discuss the film over a bottle of red wine. Gradually the talk turned to the spate of pregnant celebrities, and what their offspring would be like. Would they inherit their parents' better qualities or their worse? How much did nature account for, and how much nurture? Could you ever have it all – an interesting job, a loving partner, and bright, confident children?

"Here we are, two caring adults, and what have we got?" said Lindsay. "All right, we've both got interesting jobs, but we haven't even got someone special."

"What we need is something to occupy our minds. Some activity. A hobby or a sport. What d'you like doing?"

She couldn't think at first, then she said, "Travel. I used to travel."

"What sort of places?"

"Oh, nowhere exotic. At first I didn't have the money, and later I didn't have the time."

"How about one of those city breaks they're always advertising? Paris, Brussels, Amsterdam, you know the sort of thing."

"And you'd come with me?"

"If you wanted me to."

"Yes, I'd like you to come."

"We could pick up some brochures tomorrow."

"I never dreamt we'd be here so soon." They gazed out at the Venetian lagoon their vaporetto was crossing.

"Neither did I."

"I feel as excited as I used to on my birthday. And it was so easy!"

"The travel agent did it all."

"You don't think it's too expensive?" she asked, sounding slightly anxious. "Maybe we should have booked a weekend rather than a whole week."

"No, it's fine. Besides, we both had holidays to use up, and we'd never be able to see everything in a long weekend."

"You're right," she said. "Thank you."

"What for?"

"For talking me into it. I'd forgotten how much I was missing by being so wrapped up in work. And it's much nicer having company."

"The same goes for me."

"When you were here before …" She stopped, embarrassed.

"It's all right. You can ask."

"Were you with anyone?"

"Not in the way you mean. There was a whole group of us. Too many, really, we could have been anywhere. We'd been travelling around Europe before we went back for our final year at university, so we were doing it on a shoestring. Venice was just another stop, and we were low on funds and short on time. I remember thinking how different it was. I'd wanted to get up early the next day, and walk around by myself, but there was a mix-up with the early morning call, and I overslept. By the time I woke up, it was time to leave. But of all the places we visited, it was the one I always intended coming back to."

"What shall we do tomorrow?"

"Sit in St Mark's Square, and enjoy ourselves," he said promptly.

"And while we're doing that, we can plan our route."

"Slave-driver."

"It'd be a pity to miss anything."

"I agree. But, first, I just want to have a cup of coffee in the piazza, and watch the world go by. To let it sink in, that we're really here. Last time, we all thought the prices were exorbitant. Now I want to be able to say I've drunk coffee at one of those old cafés that surround the main square. That I've tasted a bit of history. That I was there."

"You'll be carving your initials next!" she teased.

"I might light a candle, though."

"I didn't know you were Catholic."

"Lapsed."

"Am I allowed to light one, too?"

"Without the heavens falling in on you? I expect so."

"What are the candles for? Departed souls? So that your prayers will be answered? Or thanks that they have been?"

"Probably all of those."

"I'd make a wish. Is that selfish?"

"No. We all pray to God, even those of us that don't believe."

"I suppose I should make a promise, too. You know – if my wish is granted, I'll never park on a double yellow line again." She looked anxious. "But what if I broke my promise?"

"I don't think God makes bargains. He gives unconditionally, like a mother loves her child."

"I thought you'd guess." She hugged him impulsively.

Later, lying in bed, she whispered, "D'you think it works? Lighting a candle, I mean."

"I think it does in a way. It shows you've reached a certain point where you're determined to make it happen, and so it usually does."

"Am I being selfish? I don't mean just wishing for something, but the whole thing. A child. I mean what do I know about children? What can I offer a child?"

"Love," he said. "Don't you remember your Bible? 'Faith, hope and charity, and the greatest of these is charity.' Another word for love."

"But is love enough?"

"You obviously don't know your Beatles, either," he said. In the darkness, he felt for her hand. "Love is *all* you need."

"I could sit here forever," Lindsay said, sighing contentedly.

"I thought you'd got the whole week planned. Aren't we supposed to be having a look at the Doge's Palace, visiting St Mark's, and then going up the bell tower?"

"There's plenty of time. We've a whole week."

"I don't believe it! You've been working out our itinerary like a general planning a campaign, and now we're here you just abandon the whole thing!"

"It seems a shame not to make the most of the sunshine. You never know, it might rain the rest of the week." She stood up. "I'll be back in a minute."

"Ah."

"What is it?"

"Just that, when we were here the last time, one of the girls said the facilities were tricky."

"Tricky?"

"Mmm. Hole in the ground stuff with footprints to show you where to stand. She was wearing tight jeans, and practically had to strip just so she could relieve herself. Still, that was a few years ago. Maybe things have changed."

"I hope so. Knowing my luck, I'll probably find the toilets are preserved just like the rest of Venice!"

"Come on, then." Lindsay had returned from the ladies'.

"You're not going to tell me, are you?"

"No!" she laughed, stretching out a hand to pull him up.

"Where to?"

"Here! St Mark's Square."

While Lindsay dodged the pigeons, and took photos of the piazza – the Doge's Palace with its ornate arches and intricate brickwork; the winged lion on top of a tall column; the impressive bell tower which had been rebuilt a century earlier; St Mark's

Basilica; and the clock tower – John read out snippets from the guide book.

" 'Each year, around 12 million visitors come to Venice. The centre consists of over 100 islands, with about 350 bridges, and most of it stands on wooden timbers driven into the lagoon floor.' "

"Stand over there," she directed. "I want to take your photo. I think I got it in," she said, satisfied.

"What – my head?"

"No, the lamppost."

"You came all the way to Venice to take pictures of the lampposts?"

"They're beautiful."

He had to admit she was right. The dark olive green iron posts complemented the mauve coloured glass. They'd look even more magical lit up at night.

"How about going up the bell tower next?"

There was a queue, but at last they found themselves at the top of the tower.

"The view. All those red-roofed houses. It was worth the wait."

John nodded wryly. "Even though I did have to wait nearly twenty years to see it."

When they came out, they found the Riva degli Schiavoni still full of tourists and people drawing caricatures of them.

Nearby, others were waiting for boats to take them to the island of Murano.

"Have we got time to look round some of the shops?" Lindsay asked hopefully.

"Yes. I'd like to buy something, too. Some glass, maybe."

"But you know what I'd like first?"

"An ice-cream?"

"A cup of tea! And to take my shoes off. I'm not used to all this walking."

"This is only day one. What'll you be like by the end of the week?"

"Fitter, I hope. Maybe I'm just getting old!" she teased, looking pointedly at John who was two years older.

"I'd be careful, if I were you, unless you fancy a dip in the canal."

They grinned at each other, then found a café by the lagoon, and sat and watched the boats.

Lindsay stretched languidly.

"Don't fall asleep on me," said John.

"It's all this fresh air. It's so relaxing."

"And no cars to disturb the peace. You know, we should go for a ride on a gondola. You wouldn't have to walk then."

"But aren't they horribly expensive?"

"Oh, horribly," he agreed solemnly.

"I'd throw something at you if I could summon up the energy."

"How about it, then?"

"And we'd go round the shops tomorrow?"

"You're a control freak. I'm on holiday with a control freak. I bet you eat yoghurts in date order."

"What's wrong with that?" she said defensively.

"Of course, you know what gondolas were used for?" John asked as they drifted down the Grand Canal.

Lindsay smiled serenely at him, and said nothing.

"The ladies of the night plied their trade on them. Still ..." He looked up at her. "I suppose it beat walking the streets."

"I'm beginning to think you're making it all up."

"That's what it says in the guide book. Here, see for yourself."

"All right, I believe you. Is that the Rialto ahead?" she asked, getting out her camera.

"Yes. Apparently anyone found guilty of a minor offence has to run naked from St Mark's Square to a statue near here, so you'd better behave yourself."

"Here, let me see. Idiot! They've not done that for years."

"Pity," he said, giving her a lascivious look.

"And I thought you were ..." She broke off as she remembered the gondolier.

John burst out laughing. "We'll come back here later, and see if we can find the statue of the hunchback. There are some shops on the bridge, so we can have a browse, too."

They eventually reached the Bridge of Sighs where they stopped for a moment to admire the seventeenth century white Istrian stone passage which linked the Doge's Palace with the prison. John was leafing through his guide book once more.

"Don't," said Lindsay.

"What?"

"Don't tell me, I don't want to know. Let me preserve one illusion."

"Sorry," he said contritely. Perhaps he had overdone it.

"Got you!" she exclaimed.

They both laughed, then they noticed that the middle-aged gondolier was smiling benevolently at them.

"Honeymoon?" he asked.

Lindsay's mouth dropped open, so it was left to John to answer. "Just good friends."

The gondolier nodded as if he'd heard it all before.

"My wife and I were just good friends. We've got five children now."

Lindsay picked up a cushion as she tried to stifle her giggles.

"One or two would be nice," she heard John say.

"What?" she hissed.

"Oh, nothing, dear," John said sweetly.

She hit him with the cushion.

"A woman with spirit," remarked the gondolier, nodding his approval.

The next day was warm but cloudy, so they wandered around the city, using the bell tower as a landmark, and looked in the souvenir shops which sold jewellery, glass, lace and distinctive Venetian masks. One alley would open up into a little square with another alley on the opposite side to tempt them ever onwards. They found themselves at the Rialto Bridge, so they photographed the Grand Canal and the palazzi lining the banks before heading for the shops on the bridge itself.

In the afternoon, they caught a waterbus to Murano, where they watched the glass-blowers at work.

Lindsay was quiet on the return trip.

"Are you all right?" John asked.

"Yes. No." She sighed. "I've got a headache."

"I've got some Paracetamol in my rucksack."

"I took some earlier, but they haven't worked. I think it must be a migraine, and I left my tablets back at the hotel."

"So you've been feeling ill for a while?"

She nodded guiltily. "I didn't want to spoil things."

"I'm surprised the glass-blowing didn't finish you off."

"I was glad to get out of there," she admitted. "Look, there's no need for you to come back with me. I'll go and have a lie down. Maybe I'll feel better by suppertime."

"No, I'll come, too. I was hoping for an excuse to have a nap. Here …" He rummaged in his bag. "I've got a can of Coke. Drink it – if you're suffering from dehydration, it'll make you feel better."

Gratefully she drank some, then she held the can out to John. "Here, you finish it. I can't manage it all."

Back at the hotel, Lindsay took something for her headache, then lay down and tried to sleep. The room felt surprisingly cool after the heat outside, and it was quiet and dark. At first she could hear John moving around, but then sleep overcame her.

As he made himself a cup of tea, John smiled to himself at the thought of what the gondolier would say about the two of them sharing a room. Then he sat on the room's only chair while he drank his tea. He'd intended to look something up in Travellers Venice, but soon his eyes began to close, and he nodded off.

John was the first to wake. He picked up his guide book again, and was so absorbed in what it had to say about the history of the city that he didn't notice Lindsay open her eyes and sit up.

"Hello," she said.

"Hi. How are you?"

"Much better."

"Well, just take it easy for a bit."

"I will."

Both were aware of a certain intimacy, and were tongue-tied.

"Have you come across anything interesting?" she asked eventually.

"A few ideas on what to do. But only if you're up to it."

Just then, a peal of thunder sounded. John stood up, and pulled back the curtain. The sky was full of ominous dark clouds.

Lindsay joined him at the window, and they watched the rain change from a few drops to a solid sheet of water.

John turned to Lindsay. "Wordsworth called Venice 'The eldest Child of Liberty'," he said. For a moment his eyes were unfathomable, but then he smiled. "A good thing we came back when we did or we'd have got drenched."

A few months passed. Venice seemed like another world.

They'd been watching a programme on television about a couple who had problems conceiving. The woman's cycle was irregular, while her husband suffered from a low sperm count. They'd gone through the indignities of tests and treatment only to end up poorer and still childless. The next programme in the series would follow their fortunes as they tried to adopt.

John turned off the television.

"We could try," he said.

"Adoption?"

"Having a baby. If you wanted to."

Lindsay blinked rapidly. "Oh, John, it's a nice thought."

"I think I'd quite like being a dad."

They stared at each other.

"You're serious, aren't you?" Lindsay asked eventually.

"Mmm. It was that quotation about Venice that put the idea into my head. Since then I've thought a lot about it."

"But …" She didn't know how to put it. How could they have sex when he was gay?

"Don't look so worried! I was thinking along the lines of artificial insemination."

"Isn't that expensive? Besides, we'd have to find a doctor who was sympathetic."

"Not if we did it ourselves." He paused to let the idea sink in.

"Would it work?"

"I don't know," he said honestly.

"How would we ... you know?"

"I could use a jar, then you'd have to use some sort of dropper or syringe."

Lindsay stared at him, open mouthed, then started to laugh until John wondered if she was hysterical.

"I'm sorry, I can't help it!" she said. "When you said dropper, I thought of the turkey baster my mother uses." She blinked back tears of laughter, then hugged him. "Thanks."

"You're not angry?"

"No, of course I'm not."

"I wasn't going to mention it yet, but then there was that programme ..."

"It's OK."

"If it doesn't appeal to you, we can just forget I said anything," he said quietly.

"Oh, John, I'm sorry. I wasn't laughing at you or at your idea. It's just that it came as a bit of a surprise. I think I need more time to get used to it."

John nodded. "I'll understand," he said, avoiding her eyes, "if you feel you can't."

She took his hand until he was forced to look up at her. "What is it?"

"Maybe there is a gay gene," he said.

Real tears sprang to Lindsay's eyes. "How can you say that? You're my friend. D'you think I'd mind if a child of mine was gay? D'you think I wouldn't love him?"

John put his arms around her as she sobbed into his chest. "I'm sorry, I'm so sorry," he whispered, stroking her hair.

She shook her head. "No, it's my fault. I didn't think. You've had to put up with all the prejudice, not me. I don't know what it's like, I can only imagine." She sniffed. "I'm sorry. I was emotional what with the programme, then when you suggested ... You really do mean it, don't you?"

"Yes. It wouldn't be easy. It would probably strain our relationship for a start."

"Give me a day or two just to get used to it. At the moment I don't know what I think."

"When the idea first came to me, I thought it was completely off the wall. But the more I thought about it, the more reasonable it sounded. Sorry if I sprang it on you, of course you need time to think about it. It'd be a big decision for anyone, let alone someone in our position. Whatever you decide will be OK by me, so don't worry about upsetting me." He grinned. "What happened to that cheese sandwich you were making?"

"Men! Your stomach's all you ever think about," she complained, grateful to him for the distraction.

So they talked. About whether they both wanted a child, about who would look after it, about what would happen if either of them found a partner. They agreed that their overriding consideration was the welfare and happiness of the child.

"So we try?" Lindsay asked, hardly able to believe it.

"We try," John confirmed.

"I'll need to work out the best time. How will you ...?"

"Don't ask."

"God, this is worse than an exam!" Lindsay said nervously, as she let John in.

"I thought it was just me."

"Have you got everything you need?"

"I think so. I just hope ... well, you know."

"D'you want a drink or something first?"

"No, I think I'd better just get on with it." He turned, and headed for the bathroom.

He came back looking embarrassed and relieved at the same time. "Your turn," he said, holding out a bag inside which was a screw-top jar.

"Thanks."

"Good luck."

The wait seemed interminable; he wondered if she had felt that way, too. Eventually he heard the bathroom door being opened.

Lindsay came slowly into the room. "I can't. I just can't." Her face was white.

"It's OK. It's a big step to take."

"No, you don't understand. I can't. I'm a virgin. I just can't do it!"

"Oh, Lindsay, it's all right," he said comfortingly.

"No, it's not all right! You wanted a baby, we both did. I've let you down. Thirty-seven years old, and I'm still not familiar with my own body. It's ludicrous. If it wasn't so tragic, I'd be laughing."

"Come on, Lindsay, it's not your fault."

"But it is! You managed to ... It was me that couldn't. You see, I've never even ... I should have told you, then at least you'd have been prepared."

"These things happen."

"I really did try. I just couldn't see where I was meant to ... you know. And by then I was getting dizzy. Oh, John, I'm sorry!"

"OK, it's OK," he soothed. "It's not the end of the world."

"But I've let you down!"

"No, of course you haven't. You did your best. Sometimes things just don't work out."

"I feel so useless."

"Well, don't."

"We'd got it all planned."

"Maybe that was the trouble. When the time came, we'd both got ourselves in a state."

"I should have known, though. I got so carried away by the thought of actually being pregnant that I ignored my doubts over how I was going to get pregnant."

"Have you eaten?"

She shook her head. "I was too nervous."

"Come on, then. Let's get a takeaway or something."

Later, as they watched the midnight film, John looked up. "You know, we could try something else. We probably went about it in completely the wrong way."

"What d'you mean?"

"Well, maybe we should simply have done what everyone else does."

"But could you? Wouldn't you find it … repulsive? I mean I don't think I could have sex with another woman."

"I think it might work if we were in the right mood. A nice meal, some wine, a romantic movie. Or a dirty one." He grinned, and she put her arms around him.

"So you don't want to give up?" she asked.

"We always knew it wasn't likely to work the first time. This way it might even be fun!"

"Idiot!"

"And you're forgetting that gay men probably know more about straight sex that they do about gay sex. We're bombarded by the stuff. It's in books, at the cinema, in magazines. Then when you turn on the television, there it is again. You can't get away from it. I expect I know more about women's erogenous zones than I do about my own!"

"Thanks, John." Serious now.

"I don't know why you're thanking me. It if works, I get a night of passion while you get nine months of morning sickness."

The next time was far less clinical. Instead of embarrassing individual visits to the bathroom, they went into Lindsay's bedroom together. They were still laughing over something they'd heard on television.

"I've got some ..." Lindsay turned round only to find John was holding a tube of KY Jelly, too.

"Lubricant," he finished for her. "Don't worry, I definitely know all about lubricant. Sorry, I probably shouldn't have said that."

"No, it's all right."

"D'you think that was it, then?" he asked.

"I think so."

"Sorry."

"Sorry?"

"It didn't look like it was much fun for you."

"It was OK. Much better than I thought it would be." Suddenly she giggled weakly. "Oh, no!"

"What?"

"You won't believe what I was about to say."

"Go on."

"How was it for you? Oh, God, I can't believe I thought it!"

"I quite enjoyed it, actually."

"So you wouldn't mind doing it again?"

"No. How about you?"

"Yes, I'd do it again."

"It'd probably be better next time."

"When it started hurting, I pretended I was at the dentist's, and that it would soon be over. Sorry, I know that sounds terrible."

"No, I understand."

"I suppose it hurt ...?"

"Yes," he said briefly.

"Still friends?" she asked.

"Yeah, still friends."

"I don't believe it!"

"You're sure?"

"I think so. I've done the test twice now. I left it for as long as I could because I thought all the stress had affected my menstrual cycle and because I really didn't think I could be pregnant. It must have been the first time we did it. Every time I went to the bathroom, I thought I'd find that my period had started. Even when I was buying the pregnancy testing kit I thought it was going to be a waste of time. Anyway, I've done two tests, and they were both positive. We've done it!" She smiled tentatively at him.

For a minute he said nothing. Then a huge smile split his face, and he hugged her tightly. "I can't believe it either!" he said, his face lit up with happiness. "It's ... great! It's just great!"

"I found out this morning. I wanted to tell you straight away, but I had to go to work, and I didn't want to tell you over the phone. Today must have been the longest day of my life."

"How are you feeling?"

"No different – physically, that is. That's partly why I didn't do the test as soon as I realised my period was late. Mentally, emotionally ... I feel light-headed, almost as if I was drunk. I keep wanting to laugh out loud, I'm so happy. It's the most amazing thing that's ever happened to me, and I couldn't tell anyone until I'd spoken to you. Thank God you were in! I'd have gone mad if I'd had to keep it a secret much longer."

"Hell! There'll be scans and blood tests and samples to be provided. You won't stop for the next nine months."

"I know. Isn't it wonderful!"

"Wonderful? It's absolutely fantastic," said John.

They stood facing each other, holding each other's hands.

"You hear of some people trying for ages, and we did it the first time."

"First time?" he teased mischievously.

"Well, I'm not counting the episode with the turkey baster!"

It seemed as if his world changed overnight. *What Car?* and *Auto Express* were replaced by *Mother and Baby* and *Practical Parenting*. Debates over the year's best film turned into ones about the best sort of nappy to buy. And discussions regarding the merits of a particular red or white wine became the pros and cons of formula milk compared with breast feeding.

Lindsay began to bloom, even if, as she said, she felt like a beached whale when she was lying on the sofa. John came round most evenings to help with the practical side of things or to keep her company. He was amazed at how quickly the time was passing. It seemed like only yesterday when Lindsay had told him she was pregnant; now he could see the baby move. He went with her to the scans at the hospital, and to the evening antenatal classes. Lindsay called him her partner. It was easier that way, and, besides, he was the father.

They told Lindsay's mother; her father had died two years earlier. She was pleased but confused. Wasn't John gay? They explained as best they could, but they could see she was still worried.

John hadn't seen his parents for some time. After he'd come out to them, they had been hurt and disappointed, and visits home had, over the years, petered out. He still wrote to them, and phoned when it was Christmas or a birthday, but he wasn't sure how they'd take the news that he was to become a father. They were older than Lindsay's mother, and might be shocked if they knew the full circumstances. Eventually John decided it was better to wait until after the baby was born before saying anything.

They wondered what sex the baby would be. Nothing had been obvious from the scan, or, if it had, the nurse was keeping it to herself.

"What would you like – a boy or a girl?" Lindsay asked.

"A girl would be easier," John said carefully. "What about names?"

"I thought the baby should have yours."

He didn't know what to say.

"You don't mind?" asked Lindsay.

"No, of course I don't. I just didn't expect ..." He looked up to find her smiling at him.

"I bought some wine today. I don't know if it was another craving, or just a rebellion against being teetotal for weeks. Why don't you help me finish it?"

"OK," he agreed, getting up. "I'll have to stay here tonight."

"As long as you don't mind sharing the bed with a great big lump."

"No change now you're pregnant, then. Ouch!"

Not long after, John moved in. The baby's head had engaged, which meant that the actual birth wasn't far off.

Lindsay had packed a bag, and they'd worked out the quickest route to the hospital.

"They say it's the most traumatic journey a person ever makes," she said.

"It's only ten minutes by car."

"I mean the birth, you idiot! You will be there?" she said anxiously.

"I'll be there."

"Sorry. I'm getting jittery. Is there anything we've forgotten?"

"I can't think of anything."

"Maybe we should have brought the pram home after all."

"The shop's keeping it for us. All I have to do is collect it after the baby's born."

"I'm being stupid, aren't I?" she asked.

"No. It's perfectly acceptable to be paranoid when you're expecting."

"But I'm always like this!"

"What is it?"

"I don't know."

It was the middle of the night. John had woken up to find Lindsay walking slowly up and down the room.

"Is the baby coming?"

"I'm not sure. I just feel ... a bit funny."

"Any pain?"

"Yes. That's what woke me. It comes and goes. It's not too bad. Nothing else yet – my waters haven't broken or anything like that."

John scrambled out of bed. "I'll phone the hospital."

It was a long labour. John would have felt useless if it hadn't been for Lindsay gripping his hand from time to time. During one of the quieter spells, he tried to apologise.

"I didn't realise it would be like this."

"Neither did I. Apparently you forget. I'm not sure I want to forget. I want to remember it all, but what they've given me for the pain is making it all a bit unreal. I brought my diary with me, thinking I'd be able to write it all down, but I haven't even opened it. I can't remember what we did with the camera."

"I've got it here."

She smiled tiredly. "Trust it to start in the middle of the night. I suppose I've had my last good night's sleep for a while."

"I'll be there to help."

She took his hand, and saw the nail marks. "Your poor hand."

"I'll survive."

"You've been great. Have I told you?"

"I only did what I had to do."

"No, you did far more than that. You've got me through it. Sometimes I worry …" She stopped, and looked surprised.

"What is it?"

"Nothing. Sometimes I worry that the baby will change things between us. You see, I don't want anything to change."

"Hey, don't cry! It'll be all right."

"Sorry, I can't help it. Everything's mixed up at the moment."

"I know. It won't be long now."

Lindsay managed a weak grin. "I hope not. It feels as if I've been here for ever. You must be worn out, too."

"I've been running on pure adrenaline for the last few hours."

"John?"

"Yes?"

"Could you get the midwife? I think I want to push."

It was a girl. They named her Claire. She was healthy and wide-awake and surprisingly quiet.

"Probably shell-shock," said Lindsay.

"How are you?"

"I'm fine. Just tired."

"Why don't you try to get some rest?"

"I'm too excited. You should go and have a sleep – you won't get much after they let us come home."

"I'll go in a little while. I don't know about sleeping, though. There'll probably be half a dozen messages on the answering-machine."

"I don't think it's really hit me yet," Lindsay said.

John said nothing. Lindsay smiled, and squeezed his hand. "Go home and get some sleep," she said gently.

"In a minute. It's funny – now it comes down to it, I don't know how to start."

Lindsay waited.

"You're my friend," John said at last, "and my lover. For the last few months we've been a couple. We do everything married people do."

"We don't argue much."

"Just give it time," John said, for once sounding unsure. "You see, I just can't imagine caring about anyone else more than I care about you. The last couple of months have been the happiest of my life. Look, I know this is the wrong moment to be saying all this – you're shattered, and your hormones are going berserk. It's just I was wondering what you thought about getting married. Us, I mean."

"John, you're gay."

"I know. It doesn't seem to matter." When Lindsay didn't answer, John rushed on. "Sorry. It was a stupid idea. More off the wall than the last one. Just forget I said anything." He stared down at the floor.

Lindsay took his hand. "Yes, I will marry you."

"Really?"

"Really." She looked down at their little daughter lying in a cot next to the bed. "After all, your last off the wall idea worked out pretty well."

****

AS BLIND AS A BAT

"Each to his own." The voice sounded amused.

"What?" Brian looked down and found, to his horror, that he was clutching a women's magazine that had, by chance, opened at a pin-up of a naked man.

Torn between curiosity and panic, he fumbled with the magazine, trying to put it back on the rack. It fell to the floor. They both knelt to retrieve it.

Pictures of more naked men stared up at him. He did what any red-blooded male would – any red-blooded male who also happened to be gay – he stared back. Then he jumped as he remembered the man next to him.

"You only buy it for the articles on feminism?"

"No! I don't buy it!"

"Well, I think your days as a shoplifter are numbered."

"I wasn't stealing it!" Brian said hotly, only to realise, too late, that the other had been joking.

"Here." The stranger held out a couple of coins. "Have it on me. The magazine," he added, noticing Brian's dubious expression.

Brian flushed, and backed towards the tills still holding the magazine.

He failed to notice the pile of baskets.

He hoped the assistant thought he was buying it for his wife. He wondered about actually saying that, but dismissed the idea for two very good reasons. The first was that it was a lie. The second was that, as soon as he opened his mouth, it would be an obvious lie.

He pushed the magazine to the bottom of his carrier bag. He pretended to himself that he'd throw it away as soon as he got home. All right, that he'd just read the articles. Well, OK, he wasn't a prude. Looking at a couple of pin-ups wouldn't warp his mind. Of course, he'd have to put on his glasses. He hated wearing them. The words 'four eyes' took him straight back to when he was eleven or twelve and had been forced to wear those unbecoming National Health spectacles.

"It's the Owl. Hello, Ollie. Hoot hoot! Tu-whit, tu-whoo. Twit. Twit." The chants had gone on and on until he'd hidden. Funny they'd left him alone when it came to his sexuality. He thought they were afraid of guilt by association.

It was only a few days later when he took that fateful stroll. The evening was warm and bright. Lovers were walking around the duckpond while children swung on swings and slid on slides. A steady thunk came from the direction of white-clad players practising their cricket strokes. The scene was reassuringly English.

The sound of distant shouts reached him. They were probably appealing for leg-before-wicket foul play. Luckily the distance also took the edge off the speed with which the ball had been travelling and it was only a glancing blow.

"Are you all right?" The voice was familiar. The man from WH Smith's.

"Yes," Brian managed rather unsurely. Not because the ball had hurt, but because he didn't quite know how to handle the situation.

"Maybe you'd better sit down."

There was a bench not far away.

The almost-stranger left him, consulted the others, then returned.

"I think I'd better give you a lift home."

"No, I'm fine." Brian was squinting, a common trick when he was without his glasses, but the other was not to know.

"All the same ..." He shepherded Brian off to his car, asked his address, then drove him home. Then he accompanied him to the door. Brian felt that he should reciprocate in some way.

"Would you like to come in for some coffee?" It crossed his mind that he was breaking his own rules on personal safety. After all, what did he know of his companion? He'd already nearly knocked Brian out with a cricket ball. Still, at least plenty of people had seen them leave together. He struggled with the front door key.

The other took it from him and unlocked the door straightaway.

"Thanks," he said, following Brian inside. "I'll make it. You sit down."

"OK." Rather bemused, Brian did as he was told. Somewhere in his brain, something was telling him that this was nice. Something else told him to stop dreaming.

"It's unusual." The other had returned with the coffee.

The only thing which sprung to Brian's mind was his sexual preference, but he knew from experience that people were rarely so direct. "Er ...?"

"Coffee in the container marked 'Sugar'. Sugar in the container marked 'Tea'."

"Oh. I don't drink tea, you see." Now that he had put on his glasses, he could see that the other was looking at him in a decidedly odd manner. Maybe he'd better explain. "Coffee is a longer word than sugar, and sugar is a longer word than tea. I haven't got a coffee container." Well, he'd thought it had been logical at the time.

The other nodded and Brian had the distinct impression that he was being humoured. Which was a shame, because, now he could see properly, he could tell that the other really was rather good-looking.

He told himself once again to stop dreaming.

"Philip Matthews."

"Who? Oh, I see. Brian Townsend."

They exchanged forced smiles and lapsed into silence.

I bet he'd rather be playing cricket, thought Brian. I bet he'd rather be unblocking a sink.

"Don't get many cricketers here," he said in a failed attempt at humour.

"No," agreed Phil warily.

"D'you play every week?"

"Yes. Well, in the summer, that is."

"Did I interrupt a game?"

"No, tonight was only a practise match."

"Do you bowl?"

"No, just bat. Number Three."

Brian racked his brains for something else to say. "You look nice in white." It was out before he could stop it. "I didn't mean ..." he rushed on. "I'm not ... I wasn't ... " he babbled helplessly as he realised he'd actually given voice to his thoughts. He went red.

"I'll get you some water."

Even to Brian, this seemed an odd reaction. Was it meant to cool his ardour?

"No!" he yelled, as Phil approached him with a glass of water.

Phil got his car keys from his pocket. "I think maybe I'd better just run you down to the casualty department and let them take a look at you."

Each stared at the other, frankly puzzled.

"Sorry?" Brian said at last.

"Well, it looks as if you're running a temperature and you're starting to sound a little incoherent. Maybe it's delayed shock or concussion or something."

"But ''m fine. Really," Brian remonstrated.

"You're very red and you haven't been making much sense."

"I'm sorry. I thought you were going to throw the water over me." He eyed the glass Phil was carrying as if he still thought it a possibility.

"Why should I do that?"

"After what I said ..."

"What did you say? I'm afraid I didn't really understand it all."

Brian went even redder in the face. "I said you looked nice in white," he admitted. "I thought I'd annoyed you."

"Do people usually throw things at you when you pay them a compliment?"

"No. I hadn't meant ... "

"That I looked nice in white?"

"No. Yes. I mean that I hadn't meant to say it. It might have given you the wrong idea."

"After I'd caught you staring at pictures of …"

"That was a mistake," Brian said, cutting him off.

"You thought the magazine contained pictures of naked women?"

"A misunderstanding. I picked it up by accident. I didn't notice it. That's why ... I wasn't staring. Well, not really. I was just a bit surprised. You don't expect to find that sort of thing in The Radio Times. Which was what I thought it was. I mean Channel Four sometimes have programmes about ... well ... er ..." He trailed off into silence.

"Minorities?" Phil said helpfully.

"Yes." Brian smiled. He was nice. "Not that I know many. I think I've been out with everyone I know who's gay. If an alien from Alpha Centauri turned up, I expect I'd go out with him. Although how you could tell it was a man I don't know. It's only a label, a convention, anyway. I'd probably end up having a perfectly straight rela…" He stopped mid-flow. "Sorry. I was babbling."

"I am."

"You are an alien from Alpha Centauri?"

"No. Just gay."

"Oh." Brian took off his glasses and promptly knocked over his cup of coffee. The two events were not unconnected. He started to get up in order to fetch a cloth.

"Stay there. I'll do it."

When Phil returned, he mopped up the mess. "That's it, isn't it?"

Brian peered closely at the table looking for signs of spillage.

"No, I meant that's why you're so accident-prone. You wear glasses. Or, rather, you don't wear glasses."

His one vice, his one vanity, exposed. Miserably Brian put his glasses back on. He nodded. "That's why I pulled the wrong magazine off the stand. Why I nearly tripped over the stack of baskets. Why I didn't see the ball coming. Why I knocked my coffee for six. Sorry. That wasn't meant to be a joke. I was saving those for later."

"I hardly noticed. Your glasses, that is."

Suddenly, Brian felt very happy. A smile spread slowly across his face.

"Well, say something," Phil prompted.

"I can't. I'm stumped for words. You've bowled me over."

"Are they the jokes?"

"They get worse."

"Promise me …"

"… That I won't tell any more?"

"That you'll get yourself some contact lenses. The next bright red shiny object that hits you could be a No. 9 bus."

"OK." Brian sighed.

"What's the matter?"

"I've been watching too many old films."

"What have old films got to do with it?"

"Oh, you know." Phil obviously didn't. "The ones where the hero takes off the plain librarian's glasses, lets down her hair and tells her she's beautiful, and you know that they'll never argue over whose turn it is to do the washing-up. You can't do that with contact lenses."

"You can't do that if you fall under a No. 9 bus!"

"No, I know. I'm just an incurable romantic," he said wistfully.

So wistfully, in fact, that Phil was spurred into action. Very gently, he removed Brian's glasses, told him he was very nice, tilted his face upwards and kissed the tip of his nose.

Strangely enough, his action seemed to bring Brian to the verge of tears, although perhaps he was just blinking in his usual weak-sighted fashion.

"Thanks," Brian said as he fumbled for his glasses, his face averted from Phil. He'd evidently been wrong to think that Phil might just possibly be interested in him. Had Rhett Butler ever kissed Scarlett O'Hara's nose like that?

"Sorry. I wasn't laughing at you."

Still trying to locate his glasses, Brian knocked over Phil's coffee cup, which, luckily, was empty. "No, it's me. I just hoped for something a bit more romantic," he explained, as a plate of biscuits was sent flying. "What the hell have you done with my glasses?"

"Here." Phil handed them over. "I thought I'd better put them somewhere safe."

"Oh, thanks. Sorry." He sniffed bravely.

"Shall we do it again?"

This time, Phil removed Brian's glasses, tilted his face upwards and kissed him. On the mouth.

"I'll make an appointment with the optician next week," Brian promised.

"Thank God. I don't think my household insurance would cover me!"

"Why didn't you do that the first time?"

"I didn't want to take advantage. I thought you were holding out for a straight relationship with someone from Alpha Centauri."

"That's when I thought I had more in common with bug-eyed monsters." He stared at Phil. "You know I'm as blind as a bat without my glasses?"

"That's all right," Phil said comfortably. "You're forgetting I'm a cricketer. I'm good with bats."

****

OF CABBAGES AND KINGS

It was the kid he'd seen sitting on the pavement. The boy watched him. Jan felt embarrassed as he dried his hands.

"I need the money," the boy sniffed. Jan didn't appreciate then the significance of his sniffs, but knew enough to realise he was being offered sex. He took a step towards the boy.

"Please don't hurt me!" said the boy, backing away.

Jan didn't know what to do. Cottaging didn't interest him; there were too many risks involved.

"Why d'you need the money?" he asked eventually.

The boy looked at him, and then looked away. "Sorry. I thought ..." His voice trailed off. He sniffed once more, then he turned and headed towards the doorway leading out onto the street.

Jan saw him again outside the late night chemist's. The boy was looking in the window.

"Can you buy me something?" the boy asked.

"Condoms?" Jan said stupidly.

A smile spread across the boy's face. "Painkillers."

"Shouldn't you see a doctor?"

"They wouldn't give me what I want."

Drugs. Jan closed his eyes. "No," he said flatly.

"Please," the boy begged.

And something in his expression touched Jan's heart. "OK. On one condition."

The boy moved away. "I can't. I thought I could, but I can't. I'm sorry."

"No. Come for a meal with me. Italian, Chinese – you choose."

The boy's shoulders relaxed. "OK."

But when Jan returned, the boy grabbed the bag, and ran.

Jan had been in the park the next time he'd seen him. As he read his book, he was aware of being watched. This time, the boy didn't run away, but neither did he come any closer.

Jan took out a cheese and ham roll, and began to eat, still conscious of the watchful eyes. Finally he looked up, straight at the boy, and held out a sandwich.

The boy approached warily. "Don't you want it?" he asked, his eyes fixed on the food.

"You have this one. I can buy another later."

The boy took it, and began eating.

Jan looked at the figure in front of him. Far too thin; certainly he had no need of a fat-reduced sandwich. He looked dirty, too, the fingernails showing dark against the paler skin of his hand. His clothes, which hung off him, were shabby, his shoes falling apart. Stringy hair flopped over his face; he kept pushing it out of the way with his left hand.

Once he'd gulped down the sandwich, the boy began to turn away.

"Wait."

The boy hesitated.

"Why don't you sit down? We could talk."

The boy looked around, sensing a trap.

"It's just me," Jan said.

Seeing nothing, or reassured by Jan's words, the boy moved cautiously to the bench, and sat at the far end.

"D'you live near here?" Jan asked.

The boy's eyes darted to Jan's face.

"Sorry, wrong thing to say. I didn't mean anything by it." Conversation was going to be a minefield.

Suddenly the boy smiled, and Jan could see the beauty beneath the grime. "Here and there," he said.

"What d'you do during the day?"

"Work in an office."

Jan felt rebuffed; it was probably a bad idea anyway. He began gathering together his belongings.

"Don't go," said the boy quickly. "I didn't mean to be rude. I ... walk around. Just walk around."

Jan sat down again. "What about food? Money? Washing?"

"They give us stuff, some of the supermarkets, and some of the other kids beg for money. I don't wash much. After a while you get used to the smell."

"But why ...?"

"I just drifted into it."

"How old are you?"

The boy stared at Jan. "I'm not gay," he said bluntly.

"And I'm not trying to pick you up," Jan said, although he wondered if that was really true.

"You're just trying to save my soul," the boy said lightly.

"Isn't it worth saving?"

"I sometimes wonder if I have one. It seems like just another luxury I can't afford." His eyes rested on Jan's face. "Are you a teacher?" he asked.

Jan shook his head. "Just a common or garden computer analyst."

"There was a teacher at school like you."

"A good teacher or a bad one?"

"Just a teacher. He wanted to help. I don't think he understood."

"I'm not sure I do, but I'd like to help if I can."

"Let me have some money, then."

"Only if it's not going on drugs. I want no part in your destruction."

"I'm not an addict."

"So give up. Spend your money on food. Find a job."

"I've tried. Washing up, cleaning – they won't have me when they find out where I live."

"Can't you give a friend's address?"

"My friends live in the same sort of places as me. Besides, I'm not exactly dressed for work. Well, not that kind of work. I get other offers from time to time."

Jan could imagine all too well what kind of offers the boy received. "I hope you're careful."

"You think that's how I get by, don't you? Oh, I know I shouldn't be surprised after I tried it on with you, but I haven't got to that stage yet."

"I'm sorry. It's just …"

"Parallel universes."

"Something like that." The boy's phrase reminded Jan that he was due back at two, and he glanced at his watch. "I've got to go."

"OK." The boy got to his feet.

"I'll be here next Tuesday. We could talk again if you're around."

"I'll have to consult my diary."

"I'll bring a sandwich for you. What d'you like?"

"I'm not fussy. Just as long as it's organic or free-range."

They smiled at each other, genuine smiles.

"Bye," the boy said, and began to walk away.

"Wait – I don't know your name!"

"Matthew," he said. "Call me Matthew."

"Is that your real name?"

"It'll do. What's your name?"

"Jan. My mother's Dutch. It's a long story."

The boy nodded, satisfied. “So you did bring some lunch.”

“I thought you might not come otherwise.”

“And you wanted me to come?”

“Yes.”

Matthew looked as if he would comment on Jan’s answer, but asked instead, “Is there any coffee?” He eyed the two polystyrene cups.

“One tea, one coffee. I didn’t know which you preferred.”

“Coffee. What about you?”

“I prefer coffee, too.”

Matthew took both lids off, and, after a moment’s hesitation, gave the coffee to Jan.

“No, you have it,” said Jan. “I’ll get some back at the office.” However, he was touched by Matthew’s gesture.

For a few minutes they ate in silence. A weak sun broke through the clouds, and sheltered as they were, they couldn’t feel the cold wind that was tossing around last year’s leaves. There was something different about Matthew, but Jan couldn’t work out what.

“I’ve had a bath,” Matthew said, as if reading Jan’s mind.

Suddenly Jan could see the effect wrought by soap and water. Matthew’s hands were clean – even his fingernails were no longer encrusted with dirt; his face was scrubbed, and looked somehow more vulnerable; and his hair fell softly forwards now that the grease and grime of the town had been washed out. His clothes, still tattered and filthy, now looked incongruous.

“I thought it was the least I could do since you were providing lunch,” Matthew said, and Jan wasn’t sure if he was joking. “Thanks,” Matthew added, his grey eyes meeting Jan’s for a moment before looking away.

“It’s all right,” Jan said gruffly, afraid of the feelings the eye contact had aroused in him. He couldn’t afford to let himself get involved. "Where d'you go if it rains?" he asked, trying to forget how close Matthew was sitting.

"Oh, the station, the library, the shopping centre. Some cafés will let you stay if you buy a cup of tea or something. The library's good if you're bored – they've got plenty of newspapers and magazines."

"Will you get anything else to eat today?"

"Some bread and soup, I expect, or something from one of the restaurants. It's quite a cosmopolitan diet sometimes."

"Look – take this." Jan got out a ten pound note.

"No. You were right, I wouldn't spend it on food. It'd be too tempting to use it for other things."

Jan hesitated, then put his money away. Then he realised what it might have looked like.

"I'm sorry, I didn't think. I wasn't trying to buy you."

"I didn't think you were – not for ten pounds, anyway," Matthew said, laughter bubbling in his voice.

The black humour made them grin at each other.

Then Matthew's face clouded. "I've got to go," he said abruptly. He stood up.

"I thought ..."

"I know."

"Next week?" Jan said desperately.

"I can't promise anything."

"But you'll try?"

Matthew's grey eyes lingered on Jan's face. The loneliness he saw there made him add, "I'll try. It might be difficult, though."

Then he turned and hurried away, leaving Jan to wonder whether he'd inadvertently hurt Matthew's feelings. The money, he should never have offered the money. At best, it smacked of charity; at worst, it looked like he was trying to buy Matthew's affection. And the thing was, he couldn't help wondering if that was exactly what he had been trying to do.

The boy was already there when Jan arrived the following week.

"You came."

"It was easy after all. Getting away, I mean."

"Good," said Jan, unsure, when Matthew's time was his own, why meeting him might pose a problem.

"The others, you see. Sometimes they get restless, want to do something different. It would have been awkward to explain."

Jan nodded. Peer pressure. Matthew was too young to resist it, to go his own way. And yet he was here now. "We never did have that meal," Jan said.

Matthew looked up quickly, and Jan realised that the boy thought it was a criticism. "If it's a problem, I'll understand," he added.

"No, I'd like to."

"How about Friday evening? Before it gets busy?"

Matthew took another bite of his sandwich while he thought it over. "I've no money," he said at last. "At least, not much." His eyes slid away, and Jan knew he had enough for other things.

"That's all right. One meal's not going to break the bank."

"And the sandwiches you've bought – don't forget them."

Jan couldn't tell if he was serious.

"OK. Friday."

"Shall I pick you up?"

"No!" The word came out like a bullet. "Sorry, I didn't mean ..." The sentence petered out. "It's just not the sort of place you invite people back to."

They arranged to meet in the town's main square.

"What shall we talk about on Friday?" Matthew asked.

"Whatever you like."

" 'Of shoes and ships and sealing-wax, of cabbages and kings'?"

"You read a lot, don't you?"

"Books don't leave you," Matthew replied, his face closed.

"But people do?"

The boy nodded. "People always do."

Jan wanted to reassure him, but knew there was at least some truth in Matthew's words. "We never think we'll die."

Matthew gave him a curious look. "It's not just death that takes people away," the boy said.

"No," Jan agreed. "People grow up, grow away. Things change."

"The more things change, the more they stay the same. I sometimes think everything's predetermined at birth."

"So there are no choices? We just have to sit back and let Fate take its course?"

"Maybe that's the only way. Maybe that's the problem. Am I talking complete rubbish?" he asked, suddenly self-conscious.

Jan realised he was no closer to solving the enigma that was Matthew. "Not if it's what you believe."

"But what if I'm wrong?"

"We all make mistakes. Nothing's ever black or white, only another shade of grey."

"I like talking to you – you're different from the kids I hang around with."

"And I thought you were just after my cheese and ham sandwiches!" teased Jan.

"I can't deny their obvious appeal."

"You know what they say. The way to a man's heart ..."

"Well, it's working," said Matthew. "Sorry, I didn't mean …"

"To offer any encouragement?" Jan said wryly. "I know, don't worry on that score. I won't get my hopes up. I like talking to you, too. That's all it is." Liar, he thought. The boy was becoming important to him, despite – or perhaps because of – his flaws.

For a while, they sat in silence.

"What shall I wear, then? On Friday, I mean." Matthew said.

"I don't think you need dress for dinner. It's very informal at McDonald's."

"Hello."

"Hi."

"Where are we going?" Jan asked, curious to find out where Matthew was leading him.

"McDonald's is this way."

"Hey, I was only joking. It's up to you. Your choice."

Matthew went red, and Jan realised the boy had taken him seriously.

"Sorry," they said together, and laughed, the momentary tension broken.

"Let's just walk," suggested Jan.

After a few minutes, they came to an Italian restaurant where they stopped to look at the menu displayed in the window.

"Is this OK?" Matthew asked.

"It's fine by me," Jan replied. He held the door open for Matthew.

A waiter was heading their way, a couple of menus clasped to his chest.

"A table for two," said Jan.

The waiter, after one glance at Matthew, said: "Have you booked, sir?"

"I'm afraid not."

"All of our tables have been reserved," the waiter continued smoothly.

Jan couldn't see more than two 'reserved' signs. "Are you sure?"

"Positive," replied the waiter. "Perhaps another time?" he said, trying to shepherd them back towards the door.

Jan stood his ground. "Can I see the manager?"

The waiter hesitated, then said: "I'm afraid he's busy at the moment."

A lie.

"Even so, I'd still like to speak to him."

"It won't make any difference." This time the waiter looked pointedly at Matthew.

"He probably thinks I'm your catamite," said Matthew, who'd remained silent till then.

"Your what?" Jan asked incredulously.

"Catamite. It means rent boy. I came across it the other day."

Jan, now furious, turned back to the waiter. "No wonder the restaurant's half-empty if that's the way you treat your customers!"

"Leave it, Jan," said Matthew. "Let's go somewhere else. Maybe there'll still be a park bench free." He stared levelly at the waiter until the latter was forced to look away.

"All right," the waiter said. "You can have a table. But if there's any trouble ..."

"There won't be," Matthew assured him, shooting a warning glance at Jan, who seemed about to object. "Thanks."

"I'm sorry," said Jan, after the waiter had left them.

"What for?"

"All that," Jan replied with an expressive shrug. "It was me that suggested a meal, me that said it didn't matter what you wore, me that got angry."

"Thanks – for getting angry."

"Doesn't it bother you, people treating you like that?"

"Not any more. Now I just let it wash over me. If people want to judge me by how I look, then that's up to them. Perhaps they're right."

"They're not, you know they're not," said Jan heatedly.

"Anyway, I'm no better. You must think I'm a hypocrite." He looked up at Jan.

"Because you're here, rather than at some soup kitchen?"

Matthew shook his head. "The other day I said I preferred books because they didn't go away, and yet that's exactly what I did. I ran away."

"Maybe it was the only thing you could do." They'd both been leaning forward to talk, and now Jan became aware that Matthew's hand was near his own. Afraid of such temptation, he leant back.

"It's not important now," said Matthew, and Jan knew he wasn't to find out just yet why Matthew had left home. "Let's eat, drink and be merry."

"For tomorrow …"

"Never comes," Matthew said firmly.

The weeks passed. Jan and Matthew kept up their regular meetings in the park. There were times when Jan wondered if Matthew was beginning to feel more than mere friendship for him, but then he told himself it was just wishful thinking on his part. As for himself, Jan wasn't sure when the initial attraction had deepened into something else, when his resolution not to get involved had melted under the gaze of those clear grey eyes.

"I'm going to Bristol this weekend," he told Matthew one day, as they sat in their usual place. He handed Matthew a cup of coffee, and then added, as casually as he could, "Why don't you come, too?"

There was silence while Matthew considered Jan's proposal.

"Just for the day," said Jan. "I thought I'd have a look around. What d'you think?"

"Yeah. All right." Matthew smiled, and Jan smiled back. It had been simple after all.

It was a couple of weeks later when Jan told Matthew that the company he worked for had offered him a new job.

"It'll mean moving," he said carefully.

"To Bristol. You're moving to Bristol," said Matthew, his eyes troubled.

"Yes."

"No more sandwiches in the park?"

"No."

"I'll miss you."

"You could come with me. The house has two bedrooms, you'd get away from the streets and the drugs, maybe find yourself a job. In the meantime, I'd be earning enough to support us both. I wouldn't expect ..." Jan hesitated "... well, anything."

For a while, Matthew remained silent. Then he said, "You'd do all that for me?"

"It's probably not as altruistic as it sounds," Jan admitted. "I want to do it."

In the distance, the traffic rumbled on its way to the motorway. Nearby, a little boy was playing catch. They watched him throw the ball in the air, and then hold out cupped hands. Sometimes he missed.

As the silence lengthened, Jan mentally kicked himself for handling it all wrong. He should have told Matthew from the start about the job.

"Yes," said Matthew at last. "I'll come with you."

Jan was busy during the next fortnight. Sorting out what to take, and what to throw out, packing breakable items, sending out change of address cards. There wasn't much time to wonder what would happen once he and Matthew were under the same roof, which was probably just as well.

Matthew told one of the others about Jan's offer. Davy was sceptical, warning Matthew that he didn't know what he was getting himself into. Matthew would be an unpaid skivvy, he cautioned, no doubt with bedroom duties thrown in. Was that what he wanted? Matthew tried to explain, but Davy wouldn't listen. "He wanted you, and now he's got you," was all he said.

Eventually Matthew's resolution began to waver. No matter how much he'd defended Jan, his experience of life had taught him that people let you down. People left. Better not to risk being in that position in the first place. He decided not to go.

But on the day they were due to leave for Bristol, Matthew found himself in the park. He didn't go straight to the bench where he'd agreed to meet Jan. Instead, he found a hiding place behind some bushes and small trees.

After a while, he became aware that his mouth was dry and his heart hammering, and he knew with complete certainty that he wanted Jan to come, that he wanted to see him, hear him, talk to him.

And suddenly Jan was there.

Matthew longed to emerge from behind the trees, but something prevented him, seemed to paralyse him. So he stayed hidden, and waited.

Jan waited, too. As the time passed with no sign of Matthew, he grew anxious. Once he heard footsteps and looked up expectantly, but it was just a stranger in a hurry to get to work. Eventually it became obvious that Matthew wasn't coming.

Jan stood up, and, as he felt blindly for his car keys, he looked directly at the little group of trees behind which Matthew was concealed. Suddenly a bubble of pure joy rose inside Matthew, making his whole body feel light. Jan had seen him, he must have seen him! Matthew was just about to call out, when Jan turned, and began to walk slowly away through the park.

It wouldn't have worked anyway. This was reality – the streets, the squalor, the hopelessness. How could Matthew ever have thought that it could be any other way?

****

MAKING HAY

"Whoops – my fault!"

"No, mine."

"It's just … well it's such good value."

"Is it?" Matt looked at the price ticket again. "I suppose it's not bad," he conceded.

"Not bad! Last week it was £20, the week before that, £35."

Amazed at such knowledge, Matt relinquished his hold on the left sleeve of the jumper. "You have it. You saw it first."

Gary was touched. Most convicted shoppers – no, that couldn't be right! Dedicated, that was it! Most dedicated shoppers he knew wouldn't have given up their claim even if Solomon came along.

"No," he said, feeling magnanimous, "your need is greater than mine." He saw the holier-than-thou pullover the other man wore and wondered if ripped garments were back in fashion. Had he thrown out all his torn jeans? He remembered stopping his mother from doing so on one of her regular visits. "Some of the places you've got holes are obscene!" she'd said in all innocence. Her unintentionally hilarious remark had gained immortality amongst his friends.

Matt looked somewhat shamefaced at Gary's comment. "It's about fifteen years old," he admitted, meaning his pullover.

"Fifteen years!" breathed Gary. "Then it's an antique. A classic. Vintage, veteran. Whatever. Which charity shop did you get it from?"

Matt looked even more taken aback. "Well, it was new when I bought it."

"You've kept it all that time? And worn it?"

"I don't buy many clothes. Look, you have it. I'm not really sure about the colour." It was brighter than his usual shade of knitwear.

"Yes, it's a bit dark, isn't it," said Gary, getting hold of the wrong end of the stick. He let go of the right sleeve.

"It's just that I don't go shopping much. Only when I need something."

"I don't understand," said Gary, who genuinely didn't. Shops were open far longer now, so there was no excuse. "What about this one?" he asked, trying to be helpful. He pointed to a lime-green jumper.

"£25?" said Matt. It sounded a lot of money, but then perhaps that's what things cost nowadays.

Gary understood. Matt was short of money. "Take the jumper," he ordered, picking up the original one.

The assistant approached. "Can I help you?"

"I'm not sure," said Matt. "I think this gentleman wants it, too. Do you have any more?"

"It's the last one in stock," she said regretfully.

Matt paid by gold card. Gary hastily revised his assessment, something he was shortly to do again.

He was rather surprised to be invited – ostensibly to sort out who was going to get the jumper – for a cup of coffee by someone who was so ordinary. Well, normal. Straight-looking, that is. He, Gary, wasn't at all straight-looking and knew that some people avoided being in his company for this reason. Straight men were worried that they'd be taken for gay; gay, straight-acting men were even more terrified that they'd be seen to be gay. Perhaps he was gay. Or just gay-friendly. Maybe he was bi-curious. Gary was bi-curious. Oh, not that he harboured the least interest in women;

merely that bi-curious people puzzled him. Didn't they know for heaven's sake! After all, he'd never had any doubts.

So what did Matt want? Well, Gary supposed he'd better find out. At least he'd get a free cup of coffee. (Or did that fall into the same category as a 'free' lunch?) Maybe even the jumper.

Mid-lick he stopped. The cream from the éclair tasted tantalising on his tongue. Perhaps he should eat the pastry in a more genteel way rather than as if he was having sex with it. Matt had ordered two coffees, but Gary hadn't been able to resist the éclair. The elongated, oval shape, the chocolate coating, the choux pastry which cunningly concealed the cream which was just waiting to ooze out ...

"You don't like shopping?" Not liking shopping was practically blasphemy to most of his friends. For a whole minute, Gary contemplated this fact in silence. Then, carefully, he licked a bit of cream from one finger, and asked: "But what do you do all day? When you're not working?"

Matt reeled off a list of pursuits that seemed foolhardy, downright dangerous or totally bizarre. Pot-holing, for goodness' sake! "But what d'you do in the evening?"

"Maybe a game of darts down the local."

"Darts?" echoed Gary. This was a whole new side of life.

"Bar billiards with the lads."

Things were looking up.

"Dominoes with Old Bert."

"Old Bert?" Who on earth was Old Bert? Then Gary realised Matt was pulling his leg. "I knew you were joking," he said severely. He didn't like to ask about the pot-holing. He had a feeling all that was true.

"I suppose you're off to The Orchid, tonight?"

Gary nearly fell off his seat. It was the second time in ten minutes that he'd been struck dumb. What did Matt know about The Orchid?

"I've been there a couple of times," said Matt, as if reading his mind. "Bit loud for my tastes."

"The decor or the music?" asked Gary, recovering quickly.

"The music. I didn't get to see much of the decor. There was some work needed doing. It didn't take long."

So that explained that. "I'm there most Saturdays," said Gary.

"I had a feeling you might be."

"And you still suggested having a coffee together?"

"You think I might be compromised?"

"I think you can take it."

Matt considered Gary's remark. He was about to say something, but changed his mind and asked instead: "How's the éclair?"

"Messy," retorted Gary, looking around for a paper serviette. Matt handed him a couple. Which accounted for the third time Gary was rendered speechless. Matt's fingers had brushed against his, and Gary was sure it was no accident.

"I thought you needed some help," explained Matt, a grin starting to form.

For once, Gary, master of every nuance, every double-entendre, wondered if his instinct had let him down. What was happening here? Was some blatantly straight guy really hitting on him? Or had his perception of the world become so warped that he saw everything as an attempted pick-up?

For a minute, he let himself imagine that Matt was indeed chatting him up. He supposed Matt was good-looking in a conventional way. Fairly dark, fairly tall, a pleasant voice. He gave the impression of being someone you could rely on in a crisis. Gary could do worse. In fact, he probably had. But not his type.

Not if he really did go pot-holing. So far, all they had in common was the jumper. (They really ought to get that settled.) He wondered whether Matt's eyes were dark, too. Light blue. And watching him as if he could read his thoughts.

Gary became flustered, which was really very unlike him. "I should pay you," he muttered, looking for his wallet.

"No, I said I'd get the coffee. And the éclair. I must say I've never seen anyone enjoy one quite so much."

Gary paused. Was he taking the mickey? "The jumper? What are we going to do about it?"

Matt averted his gaze. If Gary had known him better, he would have been suspicious. As it was, he supposed Matt wanted the jumper very much. He was about to say 'keep it' when Matt spoke.

"Sorry about that. You were so intent on bargain hunting, I had to find some way of attracting your attention. I couldn't think what else to do." He sounded genuinely contrite.

"But why did you want to?" Gary said very slowly.

"I suppose I don't get to meet many people in my line of work," Matt said simply.

"Can't meet many down pot-holes, either," said Gary, thinking he must remember to ask Matt what he did for a living. But first things first. "I wouldn't have thought I was your type."

"You'd be surprised," Matt said softly.

"I wouldn't have to go caving, would I? Isn't it all dark and claustrophobic down there?"

"Pretty much like The Orchid on a Saturday night," Matt agreed. "But, no, you wouldn't have to go caving," he promised.

"D'you use ropes?" Gary asked, intrigued.

"Sometimes."

Maybe there was still hope. "Would I have to learn Morse Code and knots and things?"

"Only if you wanted to,"

"I suppose you were in the Scouts."

" 'Fraid so."

"I always wanted to be a Brownie. I liked the uniform."

Matt gave him a sharp look.

Gary practically yelped with pleasure. "You wear a uniform! No, don't tell me, let me guess. Traffic warden? Paramedic? Fireman?" he said, hoping his dream had come true.

"Used to," said Matt modestly.

"You used to be a fireman!" said Gary, misunderstanding. Wait till the others heard about this.

Gary was already in a relationship, was practically living with someone. And yet he was tempted by Matt's obvious interest. He found himself confiding in Matt, telling him all about his boyfriend's childish tantrums and petty jealousies, and his own worries that things would only get worse if their relationship was put on a more formal footing.

"And the worst," he admitted to Matt, "is that I can see myself in him. We're alike." He sighed. "Don't get involved with me."

Eventually, after Gary had had a bit of a sniff, he asked for Matt's phone number.

"I can't promise anything," Gary warned.

But they both knew he'd phone.

It had taken months to extricate himself. His boyfriend had been angry and bitter and tearful by turns, and had pleaded for them to try again. Gary had given in several times. But at last clothes found their way home, arguments over disputed CDs were resolved, and friends were informed. And throughout Matt had listened patiently to Gary's outpourings even though they'd never been to bed together.

"I can't do it to him," Gary had once said. "I can't two-time him." He looked hopelessly at Matt, and Matt knew Gary and his boyfriend were still sleeping together.

And then, when it really was over, Matt had to go out to the Gulf. He was some sort of trouble-shooter. But he phoned. Gary was glad they were still friends. He thought maybe, after all, that was all Matt wanted.

When Matt had suggested camping, another of the images Gary's brain had conjured up (after delighting in the word itself) had been of the sunny Mediterranean, maybe Spain. Not some farmer's field on the rain-soaked Welsh borders. Hell, it was June – why was it so cold? His back was beginning to ache, too. "Bring a lilo," Matt had said. Gary had thought he was joking, but now he understood. At least he'd let Matt lend him a spare ground-sheet; he'd be cold and wet if he hadn't. Damn. He wished he hadn't thought of water. He needed to go for a pee but had been putting it off in the vain hope that the urge would pass. When they'd been pitching their tent earlier, it had seemed like a good idea to be well away from the 'facilities'. Now he wished they were closer. To tell the truth, he was a bit nervous about crossing the field in the dark. If he asked, he knew Matt would go with him, but he didn't like to. At least he had a torch. Oh, well. He supposed he'd better get on with it.

Matt opened his eyes briefly as Gary struggled out of his sleeping-bag. "Too much coffee," Gary explained, hoping forlornly that Matt would need to go, too. Matt just nodded and turned over.

Once back safe and sound in the tent, Gary donned as many clothes as he could find. As luck would have it, there was still a pair of gloves in his coat pocket. He put them on, then pulled on a second pair of socks. He lay down.

It was no use. He was still freezing. He sighed, and looked at his watch by torchlight. Dear God, it was only one o'clock.

"Are you all right?" Matt asked, having been woken when Gary accidentally shone the torch beam in his face.

"Is it always this cold?" Gary asked, shivering.

"Sometimes it's worse."

"I don't think I can sleep. If I read, will the light keep you awake?"

"Look, I can make the sleeping-bags into a double. That'll get you warmer."

"You promised!" Gary reminded him half-heartedly, though at that moment, he'd probably have sold his soul, let alone his body, just to be warm. Not that he had anything against sex, on the contrary; but a tent was scarcely his idea of somewhere private. So he'd laid down some ground rules along with the ground-sheet. Matt hadn't raised any objections, so Gary thought he must be right: after all those months of Gary snivelling down the phone, Matt had lost interest in him.

"I know. Don't worry, I just want to get back to sleep, too. I can't while your teeth are chattering so much." Expertly Matt zipped their two sleeping-bags together, and they both climbed in. Matt put his arms round Gary. "God, your nose is like a block of ice." He felt for Gary's hands and feet, but was unable to find them. In fact, he was unable to find anything that felt like Gary. "What on earth have you got on?" he asked.

"Everything," muttered Gary through clenched teeth. "I've always had poor circulation." He sniffed.

"Are you crying?" asked Matt in some alarm.

"No. Just sniffing. I'm so very cold."

"Poor love," Matt whispered. "Never mind, the forecast's better for tomorrow." He gave Gary a kiss, and went to sleep.

It wasn't much as kisses went.

The weather went from one extreme to the other: the next day was blisteringly hot. Gary wasn't sure if it was the scent of his sun cream or the colour of his tee-shirt which was attracting the hordes of tiny flies. Matt didn't seem bothered by them.

After a while he became aware of his feet. For someone who spent hours dancing the night away at The Orchid, he couldn't understand why a few days' walking should prove to be his downfall. He began fantasising about large bowls of cold water. Gradually it dawned on him that their rest-stops were becoming both longer and more frequent. Matt had obviously realised Gary was finding the going tough, and had decided to cut short their walk. "It's a bit hot," he explained. They both knew he was lying.

Nevertheless, Gary was grateful.

"Sorry!" said Matt hastily. He looked again. "What are you doing?"

Gary, having lingered under a lukewarm shower, had returned to the tent which, for reasons best known to itself, was now sweltering. Then, with a towel draped haphazardly over himself, he'd proceeded to cut his corns. He'd nearly done himself a mischief when Matt had appeared.

He adjusted the towel. "Cutting my corns," he said, with an attempt at dignity. First poor circulation, now corns; he sounded positively ancient.

"Oh." Matt paused. "Do they hurt much?" he enquired solicitously.

"A bit," Gary admitted.

Matt looked thoughtful. "Supper's ready," he said at last.

Gary knew he'd blown it.

Which was a pity, he thought the next morning, as they trudged on their way under a sky of grey, because he cared for Matt. He cared very much indeed.

Matt had disappeared for nearly an hour the previous evening, saying he wanted to have a shower and wash his hair. But when he'd returned, his hair was quite dry. Gary wondered what he'd really been doing.

They'd packed up the tent – well, Matt had packed it up and then patiently helped Gary with his rucksack because he couldn't get everything back in. They set out on another day's walking. Gary had mumbled something about carrying the tent if Matt got tired. He knew he hadn't really meant it, but it seemed only fair to offer. As a tent-carrier, he guessed he'd be pretty ineffectual. "I'm more a camp-follower," he quipped.

Matt smiled, relaxed and happy. "You can carry it this afternoon," he said, his eyes dancing mischievously. Gary was surprised, then decided Matt was joking.

It had to be a mirage. That was it. Too much sun the day before and too little sleep. He ignored it.

"Hay-on-Wye," said Matt.

Gary stopped abruptly. "It's real, then? That's really a town over there? I thought it was an optical illusion."

Matt smiled gently. "It's real," he confirmed. "That's where we're heading."

Suddenly Gary's spirits lifted. Shops. Cafés. People. They'd probably walk straight through it, though. And then he caught sight of the expression on Matt's face and knew it was all right. He adjusted his backpack and strode on. Civilisation beckoned.

On nearing the town, the clouds rolled away, and the sun shone down, clear and bright. It was an omen. Gary felt quite light-headed as he marched like a conquering hero into the small market town, which, to him, seemed a throbbing, vital metropolis.

His ordeal was over.

"Where am I going?" he asked, realising he hadn't a clue.

"The Red Lion. They're expecting us."

The Red Lion. To Gary, it sounded like the Ritz.

"There's been a mix-up, I'm afraid. I'm very sorry," said the girl in Reception, having explained to them that the twin-bedded room Matt had booked the night before was not available. There was, however, a double.

"I'm sorry," Matt said to Gary. "Look, it needn't be a problem. After all, I've got my sleeping-bag. You can have the bed, I'll sleep on the floor."

Images of sleeping in a real bed with a bathroom en-suite filled Gary's head. Maybe they'd even have a bidet he could soak his feet in.

"We'll take it," he said decisively to the girl.

Upstairs, Matt was still apologetic. "I'd thought it was the least I could do," he explained. "I mean, I've frozen you and dragged you halfway across the country and you didn't complain. I knew it wasn't really your sort of thing, but I just wanted us to do something together, and I thought camping might be fun. Instead you've probably just had the most miserable couple of days of your life. And now I expect you think I arranged all this," he said, indicating the bed. "They really did promise me that there would be twin beds. I've ruined your holiday for you." He sat down on the edge of the bed, thoroughly dejected.

Gary, who'd been excitedly inspecting the tea- and coffee-making facilities ("Real coffee," he'd murmured, holding up a sachet of Maxwell House), felt the situation called for something conciliatory. He sat next to Matt. "I wanted to come. Some bits were fun. And it was nice being with you."

"Yes?" said Matt hopefully.

"Really," said Gary. "I believe you about the bed. And we've still got four days left. Enough time to do loads of sight-seeing."

"And shopping," Matt said, as if Gary needed reminding.

"And shopping," Gary repeated cheerfully. "You see, all it needs is a bit of give-and-take. Do you want some coffee?" he asked.

"Tea, please."

"OK." Since meeting Matt, he had mastered the art of tea-making, too. His horizons were really being broadened.

Gary gulped down his coffee gratefully, hoping he'd never see another flask of the stuff again.

Matt watched him. "Been a bit of a disaster, hasn't it?"

"Not a disaster," said Gary, feeling generous. "Memorable, I'd call it." He was glad he'd said it, when he saw Matt's face light up. "D'you mind if I have a bath?" asked Gary.

" 'Course not. Take your time. I'll do the unpacking while you're having a soak."

Gary lay back in the steaming water. Never had a bath seemed so luxurious, so completely and utterly delicious ... He closed his eyes and let his mind wander.

Matt was nice. And capable. He'd arranged all this – the hotel and everything – the evening before and had done it all for Gary. It had been the nicest surprise Gary had ever had. But then Matt …

Gary sat bolt upright, making the water slop over the side of the bath. But then Matt loved him? That was ridiculous. They simply weren't suited. Matt liked practical things. Car maintenance. The Great Outdoors. Gary liked shopping and going to The Orchid. They had nothing in common. It was merely an attraction of opposites which would soon run its course. And yet Gary knew that Matt loved him. He was gentle, he looked after him, he even asked about Gary's corns. He cared. He'd cared enough to ask him to come away on holiday with him. He'd wanted to share his enjoyment of the countryside with Gary.

Sight-seeing. That didn't sound so bad. He'd read up the places in the guide book. Ask intelligent questions. Take some photos. They all had tea shops now, didn't they? And souvenir shops. He could do it.

Matt had a nice body, too. Not that Gary had stared, but there wasn't much privacy in a small tent. It was a shame Gary had ruled out sex, but he was glad that Matt had respected his wishes. Gary wondered whether sex was another practical thing Matt would be good at.

He found, on coming back into the bedroom, that Matt was indeed getting the sleeping-bag out. Gary was touched.

"Nice bath?" asked Matt.

"Heavenly," replied Gary.

Matt stood up. "I'll finish this later."

"You don't have to," said Gary, toying with the tie-belt on the bathrobe so thoughtfully provided by the management of the Red Lion.

"It'll only be in the way otherwise," said Matt, not understanding what Gary was getting at.

"The bed's all right, you know," Gary said carefully.

"Good." Matt swallowed as Gary undid the belt on the dressing-gown.

"Really all right," Gary added, in case Matt still hadn't got the message.

"I thought ...?" Matt croaked.

"A lady's privilege to change her mind." Gary slipped the robe off.

They stood looking at each other.

"I'd better have a quick bath first," said Matt, recovering himself.

When he returned, Gary was in bed, the covers thrown back. As he towelled his hair dry, Matt said, "How about sight-seeing in the mornings, and looking round the shops in the afternoons? Nothing too strenuous. Gary?"

He looked over at the bed. Gary, naked, was sound asleep.

****

HEAVEN AND HELL

"Are you all right? Are you hurt?" The stranger stared down at James, who was sitting on the ground.

"Only my pride," answered James ruefully. "I don't think I've fallen over in the street since I was a toddler." He clasped Donald's outstretched hand gratefully. "I suppose you could say this was a pick-up," he joked, then looked instantly worried in case he'd overstepped the mark.

Luckily, Donald saw the funny side and smiled. "If I were you, I wouldn't make a habit of it."

"I'll try not to," James promised seriously. "I think it's these shoes. They've no grip and, what with all the rain earlier, the pavement's a bit slippery. The odd thing is I didn't even fall over at the stag night last month. Mind you, I was tied to a lamppost half the night," he added casually. "Sorry, are you in a hurry?"

Donald, left tantalised by the abrupt change of subject, now wondered whether his earlier assumption about James' sexuality was correct. "Er … no. Not really."

"I know what you mean. My social life's just the same." He shot a piercing glance at Donald. "Well, maybe not quite the same," he conceded. "At any rate, it's pretty non-existent. If a couple of Jehovah's Witnesses called, I'd probably invite them in for tea! I mustn't hold you up any longer. You've probably got a train to catch."

The other man glanced at his watch.

"Oh, no! I've made you miss it, haven't I?" exclaimed James. "I'm really sorry. Sometimes I just don't think."

Donald smiled. "It's all right. I could have passed by on the other side."

"You saved my soul," James added, in keeping with the religious vein. "That was a joke."

"Ah."

"It fell on stony ground."

Donald grinned. "No, I got it. Are you sure the Jehovah's Witnesses haven't already been round?"

"Not yet, but I live in hope!" James smiled happily despite the drizzle, which had just begun.

"Well, I suppose I'd better be getting along. Are you sure you're all right?"

"I'm fine. Even if I'm bruised, I don't think it'll show!"

"Well, be careful."

"I'll try to be. You know what they say, though?"

"What?"

"The road to hell ... Perhaps I'll try Heaven, first."

"I'd try the nearest shoe shop unless you want to end up there sooner rather than later!"

He obviously didn't know that Heaven was a gay nightclub, thought James. Well, he wouldn't enlighten him; after all, you could always dream ...

Friday evening. People hurrying to catch trains from mainline and Underground stations. Smartly-dressed men and women in suits and well-polished shoes, clutching mobile phones to their ears.

It was him, wasn't it? James stared hard at the approaching figure threading its way through the crowds towards him. It was.

"D'you mind if I ask you something?" Donald said, having stopped abruptly when he saw James.

James shook his head. This is it, he thought. If he asks am I gay, it'll mean he is. And if he doesn't, he isn't. Heads I win ...

"Why were you tied to the lamppost?"

... tails I lose. His heart sank. "What?"

"Well, you said you'd spent half the night tied to a lamppost. I just wondered why."

"It was Stewart's stag night."

"Stewart's? Not yours?" He moved out of the way of a determined-looking man wielding a briefcase which no doubt contained nothing more significant than the day's FT and the remains of his lunch.

"Oh, no! Not mine," James denied hotly, as if that was an extremely remote possibility. Which, of course, it was. Seeing that Donald still looked puzzled, he added, "Why me, you mean?"

"Well, yes. It is more traditional to do that sort of thing to the groom, I believe."

James grinned. "Ah, well, the others all thought I was more deserving, you see."

"More drunk, you mean?" They were an island amidst the jostling commuters hurrying to get home.

"Oh, no, I could still stand up. Just. No, we'd been talking about the divorce rate and the number of second marriages …"

"… The way you do at stag nights."

"Yes. Well, I suppose so. It's the only one I've ever been on. Anyway, someone remarked that, statistically, Stewart was more likely to get married a second time than I was to get married once, and then someone else joked why didn't they tie me up instead."

"This was one of your friends?" asked Donald, smiling broadly.

" 'Was' being the operative word," agreed James. "Well, if I'm honest, I can't really remember. It might have been the groom."

"Understandable."

"Mmm. It er ..."

"What?"

"Well, it might have been me. The bit about the statistics. It sounds a bit like me."

"And the lamppost?"

"Oh, no!" James recoiled in horror. "I wouldn't have suggested anything like that. Well, not unless it was in the privacy of ... Anyway, it was only a bit of fun. They didn't go off and leave me or anything. They untied me after a few minutes. Am I late or are you early? I don't usually see you at this time." Damn. James didn't mean to give away the fact that he'd been watching out for Donald.

Donald didn't seem to be fazed by the remark. "I'm early. I go to weight-training on Fridays."

"Ah," said James expressively.

"Ah?"

"You're obviously someone who works hard, rests hard and plays hard. Or am I thinking of a Mars Bar? I mean if this is early and you go to weight-training, you're probably a high-flying body-builder." He sounded vaguely regretful. Then he realised he'd probably sounded rude, too. "Take no notice. You're speaking to someone who thought he should use a Nautilus machine underwater! I treat my body as a temple," he added. "Mostly because it's in ruins!"

"Scarcely."

"Oh, I see. Scarcely a high-flying body-builder, you mean? You could have disagreed with me."

"Yes."

"Yes? Yes, you disagree with me or yes, my body's like a ruined old temple?"

"You're right, the bruises don't show," Donald confirmed.

"Damn!"

"I'm trying to heal an old injury."

"Oh, the weight-training. I wouldn't have joked about it if I'd known," James said contritely. "What happened? Oh, sorry, I'm being nosy now."

"I broke my leg," Donald replied briefly.

"Where? I mean where were you?"

"On the ski slope."

"That must have ruined your holiday," James said sympathetically.

"You could say that. I never even got to Switzerland."

James looked puzzled.

"It was on the dry ski slope in Epping," said Donald eventually.

"D'you spend much time lurking in shop doorways?" James asked conversationally. It was a week later.

"Only when it's bucketing down like this," replied Donald.

"No umbrella?" enquired James somewhat unnecessarily.

"I trusted the weatherman when he said the rain was going to hold off until tonight."

"Never mind, you can share mine."

"I expect the whole of the England football team could share yours!" remarked Donald, looking at the huge golfing umbrella James held.

"Or the downhill skiing team. Talking of which, don't you have a training session to go to? With your leg?"

"Mmm. If this rain ever lets up."

"I was serious. About the umbrella. One good turn and all that."

"But you're going the other way."

"People often say this of me," James agreed blithely. "But I don't mind. My social life …"

"… Would be improved by a pair of Jehovah's Witnesses?"

"Quite. Shall we go?"

After the third occasion on which James had nearly poked his eye out, Donald said, "Perhaps you'd better let me carry the umbrella."

"I didn't realise I was so short," James said, relinquishing it.

"I'm quite tall," said Donald, taking the umbrella in his right hand.

James looked up and had to resist an impulse to tuck his left hand through Donald's right arm. For a second their eyes met.

James sighed. "Bad day at work?"

"Something like that." If he'd realised sharing an umbrella would be such an intimate thing, he might not have offered. "I'm thinking of going into the escort business. 'Umbrellas Unlimited' I mean. You could do some market research for me since you like standing in doorways so much."

"Well, on that basis, I have to say there does appear to be a gap in the market. No one else offered to share one."

"No? Well, if you'd hung around much longer you might have had a few offers. Not necessarily umbrellas, mind."

"So you've saved me doubly?"

"Don't count your chickens ... No, you're quite safe with me."

He gave a theatrical sigh.

"I suppose I'm in your debt?"

"I suppose you are. A coffee would be nice. Oh, no!" he exclaimed, realising Donald had taken him literally and was fishing about in his pocket for some change. "No, I just meant can I get a coffee on the station somewhere?"

"There's a café at the edge of the concourse."

"Right. I'm sure I'll find it. I'll probably miss the station altogether, though."

"This is it."

"Is it? I thought it was further," James said disappointedly. "I lost the car park once. Knew where the car was, I'd written it down. Just couldn't find the car park."

"Here."

"What? Oh, the umbrella. Thanks."

"The café's over there. D'you think you'll be able to find your way back?"

"Ah. That may well present a problem. You may find me still here on Monday morning."

"In that case I will definitely buy you a cup of coffee."

"A compass might be more useful."

In fact, after they'd parted – if Donald had looked back – he'd have thought James was already heading the wrong way. James, however, had decided first to buy a magazine from the nearby WH Smith's kiosk.

"The train was cancelled."

James looked up to find Donald standing next to his table. Hurriedly, he tried to hide his copy of Gay Times by shoving it down the side of his chair.

"Mind if I join you?"

"No, of course not."

Donald bought himself a coffee and returned to the table. "Typical!"

"What?"

"The rain delayed me and now I'm going to be even later."

"They say things go in threes," James put in cheerfully.

"I should have guessed why there were so many people milling around. The next train'll be packed."

They drank their coffee.

"I suppose I'd better see what the train situation's like." They both stood up to leave. "Oh, isn't that yours?"

With a sinking heart, James realised that Donald had spotted his magazine. The words *'Gay Times'* screamed out at them. He nodded wordlessly and picked it up, nearly impaling someone with his umbrella in the process.

Outside, the concourse was even more crowded than it had been earlier. The indicator board was ominously empty. A disembodied voice announced that severe disruption to services into and out of the station was being experienced. Suddenly a lone departure was announced and a stampede began. Donald and James moved out of the way.

"Might as well give up and go and get something to eat," said Donald philosophically. "Any good restaurants in that magazine of yours?"

James looked at him wide-eyed. "Are you serious?"

"You don't think I'd be safe?"

"No. I mean yes. Old Compton Street's getting a bit of a reputation. For food," he added quickly. "Well, I suppose their customers are quite often gay," he admitted.

"Only quite often?"

James looked puzzled for a moment, then his face cleared. "All right, if you want to be pedantic, some of their customers are gay all of the time. Of course, some might well be bisexual, in which case …"

"OK, OK. I get the picture."

The meal was very nice; the weather had improved; and so, with any luck, had the train service, although James had offered Donald a bed for the night.

"No strings."

"Or lampposts?"

"No, definitely no lampposts. Only when I get to know you better."

Donald smiled.

James' heart turned over. Oh, damn, not again. Why was he always attracted to straight men? Was he bent on self-destruction? He grinned, despite himself.

"What?"

James toyed with a spoon. "Just wondering if I'm bent on self-destruction. I think I'm probably just bent. D'you think Uri Geller started like this?"

"It must curtail your social activities."

"How d'you mean?"

"Well, would you let him into any restaurant of yours?"

Afterwards, outside the restaurant, James held out his magazine. "In case you fancy eating out again."

"No, thanks."

James knew the hurt he felt showed in his face.

"I meant the magazine," Donald said softly, "not eating out. There's not much point in giving me the magazine when there should be one waiting for me on the mat when I get home. Be a pity to waste a subscription."

"Hell!" whispered James.

"By the way, I've found out what Heaven is."

"I think I have, too," breathed James.

And he didn't mean the nightclub.

****

"Why now?"

"I don't know," Rob said wearily.

"Perhaps it's not what you think. Maybe Lynne just wants to move house. Maybe, now Nick's older, she wants to change jobs. It could be lots of things," Richard added, hoping to snap Rob out of his present mood of pessimism, although, privately, he thought Rob was right to be concerned.

"No, she's had something on her mind the last few weeks. I've caught her looking at me as if she wants to say something but doesn't dare. It's what I always feared – an ultimatum. You or Lynne. I'm sure she wants me to choose."

"I thought she accepted the situation? It's been three years now. It's worked all right, hasn't it? What's changed?"

"I don't know," Rob repeated. He was tired of the questions going round and round in his head, questions that had no answer. His anxiety was fast turning into depression as he allowed himself to dwell on what had happened before.

"I can't choose!" he said desperately to Richard. "I love you both, I need you both, you're both part of me." He closed his eyes, trying to shut out the pain. "How can I live with only one of you?"

"Rob, it'll be all right. But you've got to speak to Lynne. At least then we'll all know where we stand."

Rob opened his eyes and looked at Richard. He sighed. "I know. I think she might be worried that Nick'll find out. Perhaps we should have told him after all. He just seemed so young ... How could we possibly have expected him to understand when even I don't really know why I'm like this? Whatever happens, you know I love you, don't you?"

"Of course I do. But try not to jump to conclusions. It's probably nothing serious. Maybe she dented the car."

Rob smiled. "I'm sorry. I'm not very good company at the moment."

"Now don't go upsetting yourself about that, too!" Richard teased gently. It worked; Rob relaxed.

"I'll try not to. And you're right – the last three years have run far more smoothly than I would have believed possible. It could have been a logistical nightmare. You've been great, Richard. So's Lynne. You've both tried to make things easy for me, to make it work. We've even managed to sort out the holidays so no one feels hard done by."

Richard grinned. "It nearly went wrong last year, though, remember?"

"Yeah." Rob had gone to Wales with Lynne and Nick for a week, then had had to race back to catch a plane to Crete with Richard.

"We thought we'd allowed plenty of time for everything – "

"And then at the last minute the airline brought the flight time forward. I thought I'd never make it."

"Next time we'll allow more leeway. Especially if they're going to search your luggage again."

"That was the last straw! I really thought we were going to miss our flight." Rob smiled forlornly. "I can't believe how lucky I've been."

Richard noticed Rob had used the past tense. "I'm sure there's nothing to worry about," he said.

Rob continued as if he'd not heard him. "You see, I was always afraid either you or Lynne would find the situation untenable. It seemed too good to be true, I could hardly believe it would last. I was happy. I'd got it all, I suppose. And now ..." His voice broke.

"Hey, come on, it'll be all right." Richard put his arms around Rob.

"I'm sorry. I just can't stop thinking that it's all falling apart. It's the way Lynne keeps looking at me. I couldn't bear to lose either of you. I know it's selfish."

"Not selfish. Just complicated."

"But I expect you and Lynne to fall in with my wishes. That's selfish, isn't it?"

Richard was becoming uneasy at the depth of Rob's despair. He shook his head slowly. "I don't think wanting to be happy is selfish. After all, Lynne and I want to be happy, too, and that means we all have to do our share. If you're not happy, we're not, either."

"Life, liberty and the pursuit of happiness?" Rob said, making an effort.

"Something like that," agreed Richard.

"And Nick? What about Nick?"

"Children are very resilient. They adapt."

"He's got a part-time father."

"But a father who's there willingly. You can enjoy the time you spend together. That must be better for both of you."

"But am I putting him first? We didn't ask him how he felt about that."

"Nick's got everything he needs: a mother and father who love him."

"You're right," said Rob at last. "It's not really Nick I'm concerned about. It's just this business with Lynne ..." He sighed. "I will speak to her, I promise."

"Lynne? It's Richard."

Lynne had been asleep on the sofa, and the ringing of the phone had disturbed her. She struggled to wake up.

"Is Rob there?"

"No. I thought he was with you." She glanced at the clock, which showed it was ten pm.

"I was expecting him, but he hasn't come."

"He left here at the usual time." Lynne was anxious now, as visions of Rob's car skidding on the icy roads filled her mind. "Oh, God, Richard, where on earth could he have got to?"

"Are you sure he intended coming straight here? He didn't say anything to you about going somewhere else first?"

"No, nothing. You know Rob – he always phones if he's going to be late."

That was what troubled Richard, too.

"You don't think ...? I mean the roads are treacherous. It's freezing out."

"I expect it's something simple. You know – a flat tyre or something." Lynne was voicing all the fears he himself had been trying to rationalise. "Look, shall I come round?" Richard offered awkwardly.

"What if Rob turns up while you're out?"

"I'll bring my mobile with me. And I'll leave a note for him so he knows where I've gone."

"I'll see if I can find his diary – maybe there's something in there."

"OK. I'll be there in fifteen minutes. Try not to worry. I'm sure he'll turn up."

It was strange, he mused, how parks had played such a major role in their lives. It was Richard who had originally said that. He hadn't meant to come here, but, as he was driving past, some impulse made him stop the car. Knowing the main gate would be locked, he'd sneaked through the gap in the hedge. On any other night thoughts of muggers or vandals would have kept him away from the silent, exposed park, but tonight he was unafraid.

"Thanks for coming."

"It's all right."

"Would you like a cup of tea or coffee?"

"A coffee would be nice. Thanks." While Lynne busied herself in the kitchen, Richard looked around, curious. He'd never been here before, never seen the inside of Rob and Lynne's house. It was more cluttered than the flat he shared with Rob. Toys and books lay scattered about, there was a pile of ironing on one chair, and several mugs had accumulated on the coffee table. On the sideboard there were photos, mostly of Nick, and, on the wall, a photo of Lynne and Rob taken on their wedding day. Flashes of colour drew the eye: the Monet prints Rob was so fond of; a vase of deep pink carnations; and some blue cushions bright against the darker colour of the sofa.

"Nick's asleep. I didn't want to wake him," Lynne said, as she handed a cup of coffee to Richard. She took a sip from the glass of milk she'd poured for herself. Perhaps she should have had a coffee, too, something to keep her awake.

"Did you find Rob's diary?" asked Richard, anxious to get on.

"Mmm. Nothing. I didn't really think there would be – he'd have said. What is it?" Richard was looking at her in rather an odd way.

Richard hesitated before he went on. "Rob thought you had something on your mind. He was going to ask you whether anything was wrong. He thought ... well, he thought you were going to ask him to make a choice," he said eventually.

For a moment, Lynne said nothing. "No. No, he didn't. I didn't realise he'd noticed. I should have said something sooner. Oh, God, this is all my fault!"

"Don't blame yourself."

"You don't think ... " Lynne couldn't bring herself to finish.

"I wondered if he'd gone somewhere. Just to think, I mean. But it might be worth checking if he's taken any clothes with him. I had a look before I left the flat, but I didn't notice anything missing."

"OK. I'll go and have a look." Lynne put down her glass and left the room. When she came back, she shook her head. "Nothing's gone."

"Well, at least we know he didn't plan to be away," Richard said, relief mingled with dread in spite of his reassurance to Lynne only a minute earlier.

"What if there's been an accident?" Lynne was pale and her hand shook. "Shouldn't we phone the hospitals?"

"I don't know, I really don't know." Richard cursed himself as he realised he'd added to Lynne's fears. "No, they'd have phoned if there'd been an accident."

"What about the police? He's missing, after all." She wrapped her arms around herself to try to stop the shaking that had now gripped her whole body.

"I don't think they could do anything yet. Rob's only been gone a few hours. He's an adult – they'd just tell us to wait."

"I'm sorry, Richard, this is all my fault!" she said again.

"We'll work something out. We did before."

"You don't understand," she said miserably. "I'm pregnant!"

Richard stared at her, incredulous. Neither he nor Rob had thought of that possibility.

"That's why it's all my fault. I'm so afraid Rob'll think I did it on purpose. You see Nick was an ac... well, he wasn't planned. Rob will never believe it's happened a second time. I don't know how to tell him, it'll change everything. Rob'll think I was trying to drive a wedge between you and him. And there's nothing I can do." A tear ran down her face, and she turned away from this man who was, after all, a stranger.

"Lynne, it's not your fault! Of course Rob won't blame you. He'll understand. In fact, he'll be relieved."

"Relieved?" Lynne looked at him as if she thought she'd misheard.

"He'll be so glad he was wrong, he really won't mind about the baby. He'll be delighted once it's sunk in – just think how much he loves Nick."

Lynne breathed out slowly. "Yes. You're right. Rob'll be pleased. I don't know why I let my imagination run away with me like that."

Richard grinned. "Pregnant women are allowed to be a bit irrational."

Lynne smiled back. "It was just such a shock. I couldn't believe it myself. We'd talked about …" She broke off awkwardly. "But then things changed. It became too complicated to think about having another child."

Richard saw the situation as she must have seen it, and was full of remorse. "Oh, Lynne, I'm so sorry."

"You don't need to be. We had Nick, we were happy. And now this ..."

"We'll sort something out," Richard promised.

"You know it'll mean a lot of adjustments. I'll need Rob around more, a new baby takes a lot of looking after. But it won't be forever."

"We'll cope."

"And when Rob does come round, he'll only want to talk about nappies and having to change his suit because the baby's been sick over it, and being woken at two in the morning – that is if he can stay awake long enough!"

"Just send him round to me when he needs a good night's sleep!" Richard said easily.

They both laughed. Then Lynne's face froze, and, slowly, her eyes began to fill with tears.

"Oh, Richard, we're laughing and we don't know if he's all right!" She was swamped by feelings of guilt – her pregnancy, her failure to tell Rob the truth, her possible contribution to Rob's disappearance. If anything had happened, he would never know about the baby.

"I'll try his mobile phone again." Richard pushed a button, and listened. Then he shook his head. "It's still switched off." He cast around the room. "We should put on the radio," he said to Lynne. "Listen to the news. You never know ..."

"Where can he be?"

"Is there an address book we should be trying?" Richard said, more out of desperation than any real hope.

Relieved to be doing something, Lynne said she'd get it.

They looked through it together. "Who's this?" she asked at one point.

"I think it's his counsellor," Richard said awkwardly.

"Counsellor?" Lynne said blankly.

"Mmm. A specialist in bi-sexual matters. They spoke a few times on the phone." Rob had blamed himself at first for not being able to decide whether he was straight or gay and for, as he saw it, messing both Lynne and Richard about. The counsellor let him talk, let him see that bi-sexuality was equally valid, and, gradually, Rob's feelings of guilt had lessened.

"Has he phoned him recently?"

"Her – it's a woman he speaks to. I don't know, he might have done. D'you think we should try to find out?"

Lynne nodded.

Amazingly, given the time of day, Richard got through to her at the first attempt. He explained the situation, afraid she'd simply say that client confidentiality prevented her from telling them anything. She was more forthcoming. Rob had phoned a week or two earlier, and had spoken to a colleague. When she'd returned his call, he'd said everything was now all right. She asked them if she could help in some way, and then if they'd let her know as soon as they found out what had happened. Richard promised her they would.

"No one else?" Richard asked Lynne, as they came to the final entry in the address book.

Lynne shook her head. "I can't think of anyone." She looked worn out, thought Richard. The first few months of pregnancy could be difficult at the best of times, and worry about being pregnant, followed by Rob's disappearance, had drained her.

"Why don't you go to bed?" he suggested gently.

"I can't go to bed as if nothing has happened! Oh, I'm sorry, I didn't mean to snap at you."

"You could try to sleep down here on the sofa. I'll wake you if there's any news."

Lynne didn't have enough energy left to argue with him. She fetched a pillow and an old quilt, and lay down.

"I'll try the hospitals," said Richard, who, having found the telephone directory, was already dialling. He wondered if they'd ask who he was.

Lynne watched him, listened as he asked his questions, thought how odd it was that she was here with her husband's lover, and then her eyes closed and the last thing she heard before she fell asleep was Richard thanking another invisible duty clerk for checking their records.

Eleven o'clock. It was five years ago that he'd sat on this bench and spoken to Richard for the first time. Then there had been a warm sun shining down on him; now the stars glittered frostily, and his breath turned to steam in the icy air. His hands were thrust deep in his pockets, his elbows held close to his body to keep the heat in. The cold crept over his feet, seeped into his bones, pinched his face. He began to shiver, welcoming this external, elemental force beyond his control.

At first the cold concentrated his mind; he knew beyond a shadow of a doubt what he must do. Then his thoughts began to wander. Was he merely deceiving himself that they could all be happy? Had he put himself beyond the bounds of morality? Had he forfeited the right to understanding, to tolerance, to acceptance? To happiness, above all else?

When Lynne woke, the only sound was the ticking of the clock. Richard was staring blindly at the dining table. Rob's dead, she thought, and he's afraid to tell me. "No!" she whispered.

While she slept, Richard had phoned the local Accident and Emergency departments, willing them not to say that a casualty matching Rob's description had been brought in. There'd been several accidents that night owing to the icy road conditions, but the victims had been identified and relatives informed. Richard put the receiver down slowly. Rob's words came back to him: Whatever happens, you know I love you? They sounded ominous now, full of portent. What had Rob really meant? He'd been depressed, certainly, but surely not suicidal? Rob would never willingly hurt his son. Nick was the focal point, the pivot, the lynchpin of their lives; whatever they did, they always put him first. And yet, as the clock ticked on uncaringly, Richard's doubts became stronger. Perhaps Rob's state of mind was far more precarious than he'd known, the thought of seeing the happiness of the last three years slipping away too much for him to bear.

"Oh, God!" Richard whispered to himself. Then he just sat staring at the table, not seeing it at all.

And then the sound of Lynne's voice brought him out of his trance. "No news," he said wearily.

Lynne closed her eyes. "It's one o'clock in the morning. Where is he?" she said at last.

Richard shook his head. "I don't know."

"I'll make you some more coffee."

I should call Richard, let him know where I am. The phone must be in the car. I'll get it in a minute.

They sat at the table in the dining room.

"I always wondered if you hated me," said Richard, freed from the usual social restraints.

"Not hate, never hate. I used to wish you'd never met each other, though. I pretended to myself that Rob and I would be all right, but even I could see Rob was lost without you. I thought at first that meant he didn't really want me, but it was more complicated than that." She and Richard weren't rivals; instead, they complemented each other.

"I always knew I'd have to share him," said Richard. "It must have been more difficult for you. You'd had Rob to yourself for so long, it must have been very painful to accept what Rob was asking."

"Yes, it was difficult." The man sitting opposite her was sympathetic, and she could see why Rob was attracted to him. It was clear, too, that Richard was going through the same mental torment over Rob's disappearance.

"I never wanted Rob to leave you. I suppose that sounds unbelievable, doesn't it? It wasn't just the guilt I would have felt." Richard shrugged awkwardly. "I mean I never set out to wreck anyone's life. But it wouldn't have worked. Rob would never have been happy without you and Nick. He talks about you a lot, did you know?"

"No, I didn't."

"Just ordinary things, nothing private," he added, not wanting Rob to appear disloyal in her eyes. "It's just that he likes talking about you both."

"That must be hard on you," Lynne said quietly.

"Not really. It's always been like that. He's very proud of Nick."

He truly wasn't jealous, she realised, wondering if it was just Nick's presence that stopped Rob from talking to her about Richard. "He told me about the will," she said.

"Mmm."

She could see Richard was embarrassed.

"You don't mind?"

"No. You've no close relatives, then?"

"Only some cousins that I don't often see."

"Can I get you another coffee?" Lynne said, noticing Richard's cup was empty.

"OK, thanks. Aren't you having one?" asked Richard, as they waited for the kettle to boil.

Lynne smiled ruefully. "I've gone off coffee. I did before, when I was pregnant. I've spent the last few weeks trying to hide the fact from Rob – you know, tipping it away when he wasn't looking. I go for a scan on Tuesday. Another secret."

Richard looked up, concerned.

"Just routine," she assured him. "They let you have a photo now. I didn't get one when I was pregnant with Nick." She poured boiling water into a mug and added some milk. "Would you like a sandwich, too?"

Richard remembered he hadn't eaten that evening. "Yes, but only if you'll let me make it."

Lynne smiled. "I'm afraid it'll have to be cheese – I've developed a craving for it. Last time it was ice cream, so perhaps I'm having a girl this time!"

Two o'clock. He'd been sleepy then, too, lulled by the warmth of the sun. Now, more relaxed than he'd been in weeks, even the beauty of the winter night couldn't prevent his eyes from closing.

His thoughts took on a dream-like quality or perhaps they were dreams that just seemed real. Two people – Lynne and Richard? – were waving at him, so he waved back only he wasn't waving, he was skating, his arms flailing; and then he saw a child and he tried to tell him the ice was too thin but the child couldn't hear and it wasn't Nick after all, it was him ...

He couldn't feel the cold now, and yet, under the lights, the grass was still white.

"Oh, Christ, Lynne! The car! I should have phoned the police after all. Maybe they could have looked for the car." He dialled frantically, kicking himself for not thinking of it earlier.

The police said they'd make a note of it, but their resources were already stretched and it was unlikely the car would be spotted unless it had been involved in an accident. Richard was left with the feeling that it was like looking for a needle in a haystack.

"I'm sorry, Lynne," he said, after he'd told her what they'd said. "I should have thought of it before."

"Neither of us did. Anyway, it sounds like they can't do much."

The clock struck four.

Richard's eyes were bleak.

If Rob's dead, thought Lynne, Richard will have no one. "Let me phone this time," she said, full of remorse at having let Richard contact the hospitals when they might not even tell him if Rob was there, for having forgotten that Richard was worried sick just as she was.

Richard nodded. If anything has happened, do we tell them the truth? he wondered. It wasn't as if he and Rob were even a gay couple with at least some rights. Rob had a wife and child. He, Richard, was nobody.

She spoke to several people. They were harassed, but pleasant, and said they couldn't find any record of Rob. They hoped her husband would turn up safe and sound. No news was good news.

When she turned around, Richard was shielding his eyes with one hand. Not knowing if he was trying to hide tears or was merely tired, she crept into the kitchen, closing the door quietly behind her.

She must have dozed, for the next thing she knew, the central heating was turning itself on. It must be six o'clock, she thought. Nick would be up soon. What would they tell him?

"Oh, God, Richard, what if something dreadful's happened?" said Lynne despairingly. "What do I do? There's Nick, and there'll be the baby in a few months. How can I cope on my own?"

"I'm probably the last person you'd want," Richard said slowly, "but I'd help. Whatever I could do. You're Rob's family, I wouldn't turn my back on you."

They'd been waiting all night for the phone to ring, and yet it still came as a shock when it did. Lynne picked up the receiver, her mouth dry. Richard watched her face intently.

"He's here ... We'll come at once ... Thank you for letting us know." She stood there, still gripping the receiver. "He's all right," she said quietly.

Quickly she reported what she'd learnt to Richard. Apparently Rob had spent the night out in the open, and had been taken to hospital suffering from mild hypothermia. He'd asked them to let Lynne and Richard know.

Nick came into the room. "Hi, Mum. Hello, Richard. Is Dad here, too, then?"

Richard and Lynne looked at each other in amazement. How had Nick recognised Richard? How long had he known about them? And did he really accept the situation as easily as he seemed to?

Nick glanced from one to the other, waiting for someone to say something.

"Er … no," said Lynne. "Dad's not here. He's in hospital, but he's fine. We'll explain it all to you on the way there. I'll make breakfast while you're getting dressed, then, after we've eaten, we'll go and visit your father."

"OK," Nick said, as if this happened every day. At the door, though, he paused. "Are you going to have breakfast, Mum?" he asked offhandedly.

So he'd noticed she'd been skipping breakfast.

Nick had spotted them by one of the refrigerated displays in the supermarket, and had nearly raced over to say 'hello', but some instinct had made him stay where he was. The other man was leaning on the trolley, and he must have said something funny because Nick's Dad was smiling. Then Rob put a pack of yoghurts into the trolley, and they moved off.

A few days later, Nick heard an older boy telling a playground joke about three men, one straight, one gay and one bi-sexual. Nick hadn't known what it meant until then, but he immediately thought of his father.

"If you'd like to come this way."

Lynne rose, and began to follow the nurse. Then she stopped, and came back.

"Perhaps we can find someone else to keep an eye on Nick," she said to Richard who had volunteered to stay with Nick.

"Oh, Mum, I can look after myself!" Nick protested.

Lynne smiled. He probably could.

They left Nick with the receptionist, and followed the nurse along several corridors until she stopped and indicated a side ward.

"Lynne! Richard!" Rob's joy at seeing both of them quickly turned to anxiety.

"Are you all right?" asked Lynne.

"Yes, I'm fine. I'm sorry about all this. I never meant to …" He broke off. "I just wanted to think. I drove around for a while, and ended up outside the park. I was cold at first, but then I didn't notice it, and I must have fallen asleep. It was lucky that the thaw set in when it did." He half-smiled. "A man out walking his dog found me." The ubiquitous man and dog. "Lynne …" he began urgently.

"It's all right," she assured him.

"But there was something ..."

"Mmm," agreed his wife.

"You'd better tell him," said Richard.

So Richard knew, thought Rob.

"I'm pregnant."

For a while, Rob just stared at her. "Pregnant?" he echoed disbelievingly. "But I thought ..." He stopped. "You're really pregnant?"

Lynne nodded.

"But that's wonderful!" He glanced quickly at Richard, but Richard was still smiling. "Pregnant," Rob said again. "It never crossed my mind."

They talked about the baby – when it was due, why Lynne hadn't told him earlier, how she'd been feeling.

Suddenly Rob looked up at Richard. "They told me you were with Lynne," he said.

"Two heads," Richard said easily. "We were trying to work out where you could have got to. Then you turned up."

"Like the proverbial bad penny," Rob said, just as lightly. But he had not been deceived. "I'm sorry I put you through all that."

"Richard was great," Lynne said. "He knows things will change when the baby arrives, but he's prepared for that." She smiled at Richard, a mischievous smile. "I think he'd even be willing to change a nappy if we asked him nicely!"

"Hello, Dad! How are you?"

"Nick!" His mother stared at him in dismay.

"Oh, don't worry, I told the receptionist I'd come straight back. Well, is everything OK?"

Rob nodded. "Yes, everything's OK." Like Lynne, he wondered about Nick's apparent acceptance of Richard's presence. "Your Mum's got something to tell you," he added.

"So I'm going to have a brother or sister?" Nick said reflectively once Lynne had given him the news. "No wonder you've not been eating properly, Mum – I thought you were ill."

"Oh, Nick!" Lynne hugged him tightly.

"I'll be able to teach him football," Nick went on. "Or her, if it's a girl."

"Well, not for a year or two," said Lynne.

"I know that," said Nick loftily. "We could take her to the park. D'you play football, Richard? Dad's hopeless, and Mum'll have the baby to look after." Nick stared expectantly at Richard.

Rob looked from Lynne, to Richard, and then to his son. Nick had got it all worked out. Rob wondered if it would really be that simple.

****

DON'T CALL US

"He can't be!"

"I bet you he is."

"On prime time television?"

"Come in here and see for yourself."

Nick dried the last dish, and put the tea-cloth on the hook above the radiator. "They'd never have someone on a programme that's top of the ratings," he said, coming into the lounge. "Him?"

"No, he's the presenter," said Steve impatiently.

"Well, he certainly looks gay, but you can't judge on looks alone."

"He's just won a ticket to the rugby cup final at Twickenham."

"Just what he always wanted."

"Now who's stereotyping people?"

"Not at all. The prospect of twenty-odd beefy guys in a scrum sounds pretty exciting to me. Especially if some of them really are odd."

"How many rugby players do you know who're gay?"

"You might as well ask me how many rugby players I know, full-stop."

"Not cerebral enough, I suppose?"

"I've always preferred my men with the customary number of ears."

"Your men?"

"Just a figure of speech. You needn't worry."

"Why should I worry? I'm not the one who'll be forty next month. Hey, now he's won a trip to Barbados!"

"I could have answered that. How d'you get on this programme?"

"You phone a number they give you at the end of the show. Why, are you thinking of going in for it?"

"You know I don't enter competitions. The chances of winning are about as likely as a contestant on Blind Date saying something spontaneous."

"Is rugger the same as rugby?" Steve asked.

"I think so. Why?"

"No reason."

"I know exactly what you've been up to. You always do when we …"

"Most people would congratulate me on my versatility."

"Very funny. There was I, giving my all, and you just lay there thinking up limericks as usual."

"I didn't get very far. Can you think of a rhyme for rugger?"

Nick told him. "It's in the dictionary. You can check if you like."

Steve, still naked, hopped out of bed. "So it is. You really should consider going on that quiz programme."

"My mind would just go blank. Maybe if I was part of a team it would be OK, but to be out there on my own in front of millions ... Are you listening?"

"I've got it!

There was a young man who played rugger.
How he loved the rude hugger-mugger.
Then one day, oh dear! someone pulled off his ear.
Quel dommage, wie schade, what a ..."

"Why are you looking so pleased with yourself?" Nick asked.

"Oh, no reason," Steve said, casting a guilty look towards the phone.

"I suppose you were talking to Sharon."

"I may have been."

"I don't know why you don't just ask her to move in with us."

"Ah, a ménage à trois. How very sophisticated. I didn't think you'd be interested in something like that. In fact, sometimes I'm surprised we managed to end up together. I'd have thought that might have rocked one or two boats."

"Don't try and change the subject."

"I don't know what you mean," Steve protested.

"May I remind you of our last phone bill?"

"It's not my fault I've so many friends."

"Perhaps your friends could start phoning you for a change."

"Don't worry. I'll take care of the next phone bill. There's enough money in the account, isn't there?"

"Oh, yes, there's plenty in our account. The one my salary is paid into."

"Well, it wasn't my fault," Steve said to Sharon. He'd gone round to her house instead of phoning. "He'll go ballistic when he finds out."

"I thought you said he'd prefer to be in a team?"

"A team, yes. But just him and me ... He'll think I did it deliberately."

"And you didn't?"

"Not really. How could I know they were going to have a show for couples?" He looked speculatively at Sharon, and smiled. "Sharon …"

"No," she said immediately.

"You don't know what I was going to say!"

"Yes, I do, and the answer's 'no'. I thought you two were comfortable with your sexuality? Look on it as an opportunity to show people a happy, stable, gay relationship."

"It won't be after Nick finds out what I've done."

"Don't do it, then. Say you've had second thoughts. That'd be true, wouldn't it?"

"But, Sharon, the prizes! All those wonderful, exciting prizes. I want to be able to give Nick something for a change."

"It's not your fault you're out of work, Steve. Nick understands. He's never complained, has he?"

"What about the phone bill, then?"

"Everyone argues over the phone bill, it's part of married life. I'm sure you're making a mountain out of a molehill. Nick may be upset at first, but he'll calm down."

"Not before he's made me withdraw from the show. And I really want to do it. You know, last week someone won a …"

"Are you quite certain about your motives in all this? You really are doing it for Nick's sake?"

"Of course I am. Oh, Sharon, what am I going to do?"

"You've got to show him you're serious, that this isn't just some hare-brained scheme of yours."

"How do I do that?" Steve asked hopefully.

"Research."

"Research? But I've seen the game loads of times. In fact if I don't hurry, I'll miss the next …"

"No, I didn't mean that. It's basically a quiz, isn't it?"

"Yes."

"Well, then, all you have to do is brush up on your general knowledge. The library's a good place to start. You've got nothing else to do, have you?"

"I am meant to be looking for another job," he said stiffly. "But I suppose I could do some research, too. What sort of things should I concentrate on?"

"Kings and queens of England, prime ministers, signs of the zodiac, where the Olympics were held ..."

"James Bond. They're always asking questions about James Bond. Which actor played 007, who sang the theme tune, that sort of thing."

"We'll draw up a list of possible subjects, then you can go and look them up."

"How's it going?" asked Sharon.

"I'm doing what you suggested," Steve replied, carrying the phone over to the sofa so that he'd be more comfortable "Only it's not sinking in. There seems to be an awful lot to learn."

"Don't worry, I'll come round and help. We'll colour-code everything, or we'll think up mnemonics. And did I mention the periodic table? We ought to do that, too. I'll be over in ten minutes."

"No! I'll come round to you."

"Steve, you have told Nick, haven't you?"

There was a pause, then Steve said defensively, "I was waiting till I'd finished."

"But you will tell him? You're not going to wait till he's in the studio, then spring it on him, are you?"

"The idea did cross my mind."

"Oh, Steve!"

"But I dismissed it. Of course I'll tell him. I'm just waiting for the right moment."

"Tell me what?" said a voice.

Steve looked up to find Nick standing in the doorway. He gave what he hoped was a reassuring smile. "Got to go now," he said to Sharon. "See you in a quarter of an hour." He put the receiver down. "It was just about that job I had the interview for," Steve said. "I didn't get it."

"Never mind. Something'll turn up."

"Mr Micawber in David Copperfield," Steve said promptly.

Well, he'd done the easy part: heads of state, capital cities, space missions; and he could now name the world's longest river, highest mountain and fastest animals. After much effort, he'd even managed to commit to memory the planets in their order from the sun. Now came the hard part.

"You've what?" Nick yelled.

Steve repeated what he'd said. To his amazement, Nick suddenly smiled.

"It's a joke, right?"

"No. they're recording the show next week. It'll be broadcast a couple of days later."

"Why didn't you tell me?"

"Because I knew you'd get upset."

"Upset? Upset? I'm livid! I told you I don't go in for competitions."

"I didn't think we'd get chosen."

"I suppose that's why you phoned them in the first place!"

"It'll be all right. Sharon's been helping me."

"I knew you two were up to something. I thought you were just planning a surprise party."

"Don't worry, I won't let you down."

"Oh, Steve, it's not that."

"Is it because we're gay? I thought you didn't mind people knowing."

"Telling our families and friends is one thing, telling the whole world is something else."

"I'll ask Sharon if she'll do it. Maybe she'll agree this time," Steve said dejectedly.

Nick watched him as he began to dial. He sighed. "OK, you win. I'll do it."

"He's doing it for you, you know," Sharon said to Nick. She'd come round to see Steve, but he wasn't back from the library yet.

"For me?"

"Yes. He wants to express his appreciation, to show he's not taking you for granted. Not having a job's beginning to get to him. He wants to prove he can do something. He doesn't want to be a burden."

"I don't think of him as a burden. Whatever gave him that idea?"

"I think the phone bill tipped the balance."

"I was joking, I thought he knew that."

"He probably does, but subconsciously he's afraid he's not pulling his weight. He really wants to win for your sake. That's why he's been spending so much time at the library just lately. Anyway, no one'll know that you're gay. They just want two people competing as a team. You can be as discreet as you like."

"Oh, it's not that that's bothering me."

"But Steve said …"

"I just let him think that."

"So what is it, then?"

"All those people ... I'm afraid we'll make fools of ourselves."

"Don't underestimate Steve – he's been working really hard."

"I know he has. That makes it even worse. If I ask him to pull out, all that work will have been for nothing. And if I let him go ahead with it ... I fell over, you know. Going down the steps after collecting a cup on prize-giving day. The whole school laughed at me. I've seen the show. The contestants have to walk down some stairs. I don't think I can do it."

"Have you told Steve about the incident at school?"

"No, it still makes me cringe."

"You should tell him. Anyway, you'll cope. You're grown up now, it'd be different."

"Yeah," he said glumly. "Instead of embarrassing myself in front of a few hundred people, now I can do it in front of millions."

The day of the recording dawned bright and clear. Nick was up early. He made himself some coffee and toast, then wondered if he should go easy on the coffee. It was eight o'clock and the postman had been before Steve came down, his eyes shining excitedly.

"Well, today's the day!"

Nick smiled, and hoped Steve couldn't see how nervous he was.

"Thanks," said Steve.

"What for?"

"For understanding. I really thought you'd hit the roof. And then I've been out all the time, either at the library or round at Sharon's. You know you don't have to go through with it. I won't mind."

"I'll be all right. Don't worry."

"Well, if you're sure ... Hey, what prizes d'you think they'll have this week?"

"Juliet," said Nick.

"Bravo," said Steve.

"Foxtrot."

"Tango."

"Lima."

"Peru."

"I'm sorry," said the quiz-master. "The answer is 'piper'."

While the compere ran through the list of prizes they had won, Steve looked regretfully at the shiny red car that would never be parked in their driveway.

"Sorry," he said, as they hung around in Hospitality after the show. There was a buffet, but he was too depressed to eat.

"At least I didn't fall down the stairs," said Nick. "Oh, this came for you earlier. I didn't mean to open it, but I was in such a state that I didn't notice it was addressed to you." He handed an envelope to Steve.

Steve read the letter slowly, then looked up. "You know what it says? And you still went through with it, even though you were terrified?"

"I knew how hard you'd worked. I didn't want you to be disappointed."

"We didn't win the car."

"I don't care about the car, but I am glad you've got a job at last."

Steve grinned. "I'll be able to pay the phone bills myself now."

"Forget the bills, I never really minded. It's a pity, though," Nick said thoughtfully. "What with your new job, you won't have so much time to spend on the phone."

"That's where you're wrong. I'll be able to spend as much time as I like on the phone. My new job – it's at a call centre. Now, Nick, put down that vol-au-vent!"

****

THE GYM

Ross stopped dead. It was unbelievable – all those men, all those rippling muscles, all that complicated apparatus. It was a dream come true and yet it was a nightmare. Perhaps he should go now before it was too late. After all, he was practically a seven-stone weakling. His presence here would dramatically lower the testosterone average. He must have been out of his mind even to consider weight-training; he should have opted for badminton – at least he had the right physique for that. Just as he was about to turn away, one of the men glanced up and smiled at him.

He was everything he'd ever dreamt of. And he was here.

"Looking for someone?"

"Yes. No. I ... Is there a teacher or someone?" Oh, God, this was worse than he'd imagined. It was the pheromones.

"Yes, over there."

Ross looked where the other pointed. A dauntingly fit young man was showing another equally healthy specimen of manhood how to use one of the contraptions. Ross was irresistibly reminded of the dentist's. That frightened him, too.

"I just ... "

"D'you want me to show you the ropes?"

Thinking for a minute he meant more equipment, Ross stared around.

Another smile split the stranger's face.

"Come on. Have a go on this. I'll adjust it for you. First time?" He got off whatever it was he was on. To Ross, it seemed like some mediaeval instrument of torture. Which was probably how it would feel.

"Yeah," Ross said, remembering just in time.

His hands were so close, so gentle ...

"Like this."

"Oh. Aargh!"

"Careful!"

"Sorry." Damn.

He hoped the trainer wouldn't come over. It was too good an opportunity to let slip.

"Take it slowly today," the other man, who'd introduced himself as Greg, said.

"Don't you have to be getting back to your own exercise programme?" Ross asked eventually. "Instead of helping me?"

"Yes, I suppose I'd better. Give me a shout if you get stuck."

"OK."

"Anytime."

While Ross exercised, he couldn't help looking in the wall mirror to see how the other man was doing. Ross sighed; he made it look so easy. Ross wondered if he'd ever end up with muscles like those. He didn't think so.

"Coming next week?" asked his knight in shining armour.

"Probably."

"We haven't scared you off, then?"

Ross grinned. "It was quite good fun, really."

"Some of us go for a drink afterwards in the bar upstairs. You're welcome to join us."

Ross was touched. He nodded. "OK."

"The showers are this way."

Showers? Ross was aghast. "I haven't got a towel," he said wildly. "Anyway, I'm not too hot and sweaty. Not that I meant to imply ..."

Greg laughed. "No, I am definitely hot and sweaty. OK, see you in ten minutes. You'll be all right?"

Ross nodded. "Can I get you a drink?"

"That would be great. An orange juice, please."

"OK."

Greg watched as Ross walked to the double doors and made a complete pig's ear of opening the right one the right way. Then he smiled and went for a shower.

"Hello," the others said, joining them. Sports bags were put on the floor, and glasses containing soft drinks on the table.

"Wasn't too bad, was it?" someone asked.

Ross smiled. "I'll tell you tomorrow."

The others laughed.

"Sorry, I didn't catch your name," said Stuart.

"Ross."

"Roth?" Puzzled.

"Yes." Only it came out as 'yeth'.

Embarrassment at what was clearly a speech impediment made the others busy themselves with their drinks and needlessly adjust beer mats.

"By the end of the session, you were doing really well," said Greg quickly.

"Thank you. When I came in, it looked really space-age. I was terrified."

"Everyone panics when they first see the equipment. Most of it's quite easy once someone shows you how it works."

"Have you been coming here long?" asked Ross.

"Greg has," Stuart said. "He roped us in. At the start, we were all flab. Now look at us!"

Ross risked a quick assessment. Even now that they were wearing shirts and sweaters, they still looked muscular to him. "I haven't even got any flab," he sighed.

Greg smiled at him. "Don't worry, you look all right. We can't all be Charles Atlas."

Ross smiled back. Despite his size, Greg was extraordinarily nice.

They talked and sipped their drinks. Eventually, Ross looked at his watch. He stood up.

"Are you going?" one of the others asked.

"I'll miss my bus otherwise," he said, in a sentence abounding with pitfalls for those who lisp.

"Greg'll give you a lift, won't you, Greg?"

Ross looked at Greg awkwardly. As it was, he felt he'd imposed. "I don't want to take you out of your way," he said.

"It's no trouble," Greg assured him.

"It's all right – he doesn't bite."

"And it's not as if he's gay," someone else added.

"Take no notice," said Greg. "They're just trying to be funny." He'd noticed Ross's reaction, however.

"OK. Thank you."

It was settled.

Outside, Greg toyed with his car keys. "Sorry about that. You were rather steamrollered into accepting a lift. I'll understand if you'd rather not go with me."

Again, Ross was moved. How could he refuse? Greg had shown him nothing but kindness. "Of course I'll come."

"Are you always this quiet?" Greg asked once they were in the car.

"No. It's just ..." Ross shrugged.

"Difficult?"

"Mmm."

"I s'pose meeting new people can be a bit of a trial. Not knowing whether things'll be OK."

Ross was surprised at his perception. "You're right. I try to watch what I say, but it's not always easy. I get nervous and come out with the wrong thing."

"Don't worry about the others. They're all right once you get to know them." Greg smiled.

"I've come across worse," Ross admitted. "There's a lot of …"

"Prejudice?"

"I suppose you could call it that. People assume things about you. They jump to conclusions."

"Yes," said Greg feelingly.

Ross frowned, uncomprehending.

"Because I'm built the way I am, people think either that I'm stupid or that I'm spoiling for a fight," Greg explained.

"And you're neither," Ross said quietly.

"No. I'd just like to keep in shape." He gave Ross a broad smile. "So how long have you known?"

"Oh, ever since I began to talk."

Suddenly there was an awkward silence. They both realised they'd been at cross-purposes.

"I'm sorry," apologised Greg. "I thought ... Look, if I've jumped to the wrong conclusion like everyone else ..."

Ross surprised him by laughing. "No, of course you haven't. I'm gay. That's what you meant, isn't it?"

"Yes. And you thought ..."

"... It was my lisp you meant. That was me jumping to conclusions."

"I'm sorry, I should have known. You're very sensitive about it, aren't you?"

Ross nodded. "Yeah. I expect I know all the synonyms for words beginning with 's'. And for some ending in an 's'. My name's the worst."

"Ross isn't too bad."

"I haven't told you my last name."

"Let's hear it then."

"Thayerth."

It took Greg a moment to work it out. Sayers. "Yes, I see what you mean. It must have made life hell."

"You could say that. I've toyed with the idea of changing it by deed poll."

"What's stopped you?"

"I don't know, really. People tell me they get used to it, that it doesn't bother them. I think it bothers me more." He smiled.

"What is it?"

"Sometimes it may even make life easier. At least I don't have to try to say I'm straight!" They both laughed.

"By the way," Greg said, "the showers are perfectly respectable. Dividers, curtains, that sort of thing."

"Oh. Good. Pretty obvious, huh?"

"It's not a crime to be shy."

"No, I suppose not. If it was just shyness." His lips twitched.

"Wash your mouth out!" commanded Greg.

"You must have a dirty mind, too, to know what I was thinking!"

Greg laughed good-naturedly. "Very probably."

And so Ross continued going to weight-training sessions. He enjoyed them. And, if he was being honest, he enjoyed the atmosphere. And drinks in the upstairs bar. The others were friendly; Greg, especially, was very easy-going. He'd been collecting Ross and taking him home again. Ross made sure he bought the drinks. It was an arrangement that seemed to suit both parties.

On this particular evening, they'd arrived earlier than usual, and the gym was empty.

"I suppose we'd better wait for the trainer," said Ross.

"Or do a few warm-up exercises."

"Mmm."

For some reason, they felt reluctant to start.

He looked at him. He was the sort of person he'd always dreamed of. Suddenly, he found himself kissing him.

That was when the others walked in.

"I'm sorry. I'm really sorry," said Ross, backing away from Greg, but addressing all of them. "It was all my fault. I didn't mean to ..." He bolted for the door, this time managing to open it straightaway.

Greg found him a few minutes later at the bus stop.

"Hop in," he said. He'd brought the car round.

Ross got in without a word.

Greg had intended driving back to Ross's house, but, distracted, found they had ended up outside his own.

"Would you like to come in for a coffee?" he asked.

Ross just nodded.

Greg made the coffee and brought in the mugs.

"I'm sorry. I got ... carried away."

"Don't worry. I quite enjoyed it. Did you see the look on their faces?"

"Yes. Are we still friends?"

"Of course. Actually …" He put down his mug and looked directly into the other's eyes. "I was hoping we could be more than just friends."

Afterwards, Ross lay warm and relaxed and happy in Greg's big double bed. Greg was getting dressed. Content, Ross watched him.

"You really have got an amazing body," Ross said.

"Oh, it comes from spending so much time at the gym." Then Greg realised Ross didn't mean his upper torso. "Oh." He smiled. "Thanks." He sat down on the bed and took Ross's hand. "It's funny: I didn't think you'd be interested in a muscle-bound lout like me."

"It just goes to show you should never jump to conclusions," said Ross softly. "Maybe I just happen to like muscle-bound louts," he teased.

After a minute, Greg said: "Time to get up."

Ross smiled like a cat who's found the cream. "There's no hurry, is there?" He stretched luxuriously.

Greg grinned from ear to ear. "I said we'd meet the others in the bar at ten."

"You're joking!"

Greg shook his head. "It's Stuart's birthday. We can't not go."

"But ... They'll know what we've been doing. We can't ..."

Greg just smiled infuriatingly at him.

Which is why Ross found himself back at the sports centre again.

"Sorry we're late," said Greg.

"That's all right. I mean, it's only my birthday. Nothing special. Besides, I expect you had your own celebration."

Ross looked daggers at Greg who had the grace to blush.

"That's it!" exclaimed Stuart. "The sods have had their own workout! Bloody hell."

"Take no notice," Greg said to Ross. "They're just jealous."

"On my birthday!" wailed Stuart. "They couldn't even wait!"

Puzzled, but relieved, Ross realised the others had accepted the situation. He could put up with a bit of leg-pulling.

"You could have told us you were gay," Stuart complained.

Ross looked at Greg, then noticed the others were all looking, not at Greg, but at him. Him.

That night, as they lay in bed, he let his mind drift back to their first meeting ...

He was everything he'd ever dreamt of. And he was here. His hands were so close, so gentle ... He hoped the trainer wouldn't come over. It was too good an opportunity to let slip.

He remembered earlier that evening when the desire to steal a kiss had become irresistible ...

Greg smiled tenderly at the lithe body fast asleep beside him. One day soon, he would tell Ross. One day.

****

INVITATION TO DINE

He read the ads again. Four. A good number. Four not-so-young men, vulnerable yet somehow still optimistic, looking for their soul mate. He smiled to himself. If he acted quickly enough, his plan might just work.

He pulled the phone towards him and dialled the first of the numbers. Working steadily, he'd soon left the same message for all of them. He wondered how many would accept his invitation.

Over the course of the next few days, he had three replies. Two accepted immediately, while one was unsure and wanted more information. The man was happy to oblige. Number three on his list hadn't responded by the end of the week, and the man was becoming concerned. Should he call the whole thing off, or should he try to find someone else? He was loath to abandon his mission, which he'd been planning for months and for which, as if on cue, the local newspaper's lonely hearts column had suddenly, miraculously, yielded the right participants. It could be weeks before the circumstances were so auspicious again. He was reluctantly beginning to admit to himself that he'd have to postpone the events he'd arranged when number three contacted him.

"Sorry, I've been away. Am I too late?"

Of course, the man realised they'd be suspicious – anyone with an ounce of common sense would be – so he'd written the note which the waiter delivered to their table once all four had arrived. It simply said that its writer hoped they would spend an enjoyable evening in each other's company; if they were at all concerned, the owner of the restaurant would vouch for the writer, who apologised for interfering in their lives in this unconventional fashion.

The four men discussed it between themselves, and soon realised that they'd taken all reasonable precautions. None of them had given their surname, telephone number or address to the mystery caller; and all had told someone where they'd be. They each had a mobile phone, and Mike, although he didn't volunteer the fact, was also carrying a personal alarm. Stephen's brother was collecting him at the end of the evening, while the others had already arranged to be picked up by taxis from reputable companies.

They decided to stay. After all, it was an intriguing situation.

The man turned away, pleased with the way things were going. He'd brought them together, but now it was up to them.

At first, all four had joined in the general conversation, but then they'd split naturally into pairs: Raymond with Stephen, and Dave with Mike.

"Which one are you?" Dave asked Mike. They'd quickly worked out that their advertisements had all appeared in the same issue of the local paper.

Mike pointed to the ad which read: Gay guy, 40s, sincere, loving and gentle, would like to meet a nice guy for friendship and perhaps romantic times. He smiled, somewhat embarrassed.

"What made you advertise?" asked Dave sympathetically.

"My friends talked me into it. My partner died three years ago."

"You must miss him. I'm sorry, I know that's inadequate."

Mike hesitated, then plunged on. "I miss the companionship, being part of a couple, waking up next to someone. I've had three years of grieving, but now I'm just ... lonely. I don't want to spend the rest of my life looking back. If there's one thing James's death taught me, it's that life's too precious to waste." He had to move on, even if he never found anyone to love as much as he'd loved James.

"It was AIDS," he added quietly.

"Yeah, I guessed."

"Meeting Cassie helped."

"Cassie?"

"Yes. She's an interior designer. We'd talked – me and James – about having the flat redecorated, but then other things took priority, and we never got round to it. While we were in Manchester – that's where James's family live – we'd let the flat. When I came home by myself it seemed even more depressing than ever. I had to do something."

Mike hadn't been sure whether he could afford an interior designer – while he and James had been in Manchester, Mike hadn't worked much and his savings had dwindled at an alarming rate – but Cassie had been persuasive and her rates reasonable.

"We took to each other right away. After I'd explained that I'd always wanted somewhere light and airy, I started to tell her about James. She listened and she sympathised and she understood about the flat." She'd found his paintings, too. He'd almost forgotten about them, it had been so long since he'd done anything. But he knew that, once she'd gone, he'd get out his paints, and see whether the urge to put brush to paper was still there.

"Why did you put an ad in the paper, then?" Mike asked, having said more than he'd intended to, and afraid he'd been monopolising the conversation.

"I hoped this time I'd meet someone interesting."

"And instead you met me!"

They grinned at each other.

"This isn't the first time, then?" asked Mike.

"No," Dave admitted. So far, the only people he'd met had fallen into two categories: the desperate, and the promiscuous. He hoped he himself wasn't the first, although now that his fortieth birthday was fast approaching he'd begun to wonder whether his subconscious was kicking in.

"What sort of person are you looking for?" Mike prompted.

"I've been asking myself that. I suppose someone who shares my sense of humour. A few years ago I'd have said someone I'd fall madly in love with, but maybe my expectations were unrealistic. Now I'm prepared to settle for a relationship based on mutual liking. Surely there must be someone out there!"

Mike smiled at Dave. "You don't remember me, do you?" he asked.

Dave looked more closely at him. Could he have slept with Mike and forgotten? In his younger days, he'd flitted from partner to partner, preferring the thrill of the chase to the intimacy of a long-term relationship. He was well aware that he'd been one of the lucky ones.

As if reading his mind, Mike said: "No, we never went to bed together. That was the problem."

"I was an idiot," Dave admitted. "Totally insensitive. And only after one thing. I hope I've grown up since then."

"Maybe I should have taken you up on your offer. When I met James, he was already HIV positive, so we never ..." He shrugged.

For a moment, Dave didn't fully understand the implications, but then he realised that Mike and James had loved each other. It was as simple and as complicated as that. He looked at Mike with respect, envying the closeness he and James had obviously shared.

"Being a forty-two-year-old virgin is something of an embarrassment," Mike said lightly.

Raymond and Stephen had been swapping life histories, too. Raymond had been in a relationship until his partner had left him for a younger model.

"Quite literally," he explained wryly. The 'other man' was an eighteen-year-old photographic model with a pretty face and youth and vitality on his side. "I didn't stand a chance. With hindsight, I should have realised what was happening. My partner had changed his image, his deodorant and then his car. I didn't realise I'd be next on the list until I found him packing.

"He told me not to worry about the rest of his things – he'd come back for them later.

"I briefly considered snipping off all the sleeves and trouser legs of his new suits, even though that seemed like sacrilege to me, or taking them round to the nearest charity shop, but I knew I didn't have the energy required for such acts of revenge. I applied for, and was granted, custody of the cat. My ex-partner's new boyfriend suffers from asthma, and didn't want the animal in his dust-free, minimalist loft." Suddenly he grinned mischievously. "I can't help wondering whether the boyfriend will put up with Clive cutting his toenails in bed!" Raymond laughed, obviously over the worst of the break-up, and Stephen joined in.

"Look – that's me," said Raymond, pointing to the lonely hearts page.

Mike read, Gay guy, 40, loving, caring and honest, seeks similar for fun, friendship, hopefully relationship.

"Your turn now."

"Well," began Stephen, after a moment's reflection, "I'm forty-three years old, and I'm a doctor. I like gardening and going to art galleries."

"What made you decide to write to the newspaper?"

Stephen looked sheepish. "It all started when my brother – he's in his forties, too – got married. We're all late starters in our family. He suggested that, if I planned on doing something similar, then I'd better get a move on. I said I was perfectly happy with my present lifestyle. Famous last words.

"A couple of weeks later I woke up to find that I did want more from life. Until I was thirty, I'd spent most of my time either studying or working. If I wanted company, I had quite a wide circle of friends I visited exhibitions or the theatre with. When I wanted solitude, I would do some gardening. It let me work off some physical energy, and I could let my mind drift.

"There'd been a male nurse I'd been fond of, but nothing had come of it." Both of them had been too wary of the consequences, over-conscious of the hierarchical structure of the hospital. And Stephen had been too young to appreciate that this might indeed be his chance of love. "The nurse moved back up north where he eventually met his partner. They must have been together for five years now. I still get a card at Christmas, but now it's signed from both of them."

Now they were on to work.

"It's a bit of a cheek, calling myself a fashion designer," Raymond was saying. "It's just a two-man band, only the other man's actually a woman. We do everything – choosing the fabric, the shade and the pattern, working out the design. I even do the cutting out and stitching."

"I suppose it's a bit like being a surgeon," said Stephen.

"Um ... yes, I suppose so."

They stared at each other. After a few seconds, they both burst out laughing.

"I'm sorry!" said Stephen, wiping his eyes. "I don't know what made me say such a stupid thing!"

"It's this wine – it's quite strong."

Stephen shook his head. "No, it's me. I don't usually do this sort of thing."

"What – eat out?"

"Go on dates. If this is a date. I'm not used to being with other gay people."

"You go to art galleries with straight friends?"

"Yes," said Stephen rather apologetically before he noticed Raymond's expression.

"I'm sorry, I just couldn't resist it after what you said."

"They're very nice people."

"I'm sure they are."

"You'll like them."

This time it was Raymond's turn to be thrown. "You're asking me?"

"Yes. Or aren't you used to straight people?" Stephen enquired innocently.

They'd certainly enjoyed themselves, the waiter thought as he was locking up later that evening. That was what he liked about the job, even if the hours were long. In fact, tonight things had been almost back to normal. Old Mr Rossi, the owner, had smiled and joked and seemed to have recovered his usual good humour. He wondered if it was something to do with that note he had given him to deliver.

Mr Rossi looked through the album at the photos of his son. The last one had been taken two years earlier, and he'd never been able to look at it without thinking of the letter his son had written before taking his own life. Now the awful guilt he'd felt on learning how lonely his son had been seemed to have gone.

He shut the album slowly.

****

ATLANTIC DRIFT

The following are extracts from some of the emails and telephone conversations between Alex and Andrew. There were, however, many more communications between the two.

Email between Alex and Andrew on Sunday 15th March 1998:

"Anyone out there?"

"Me."

"Hi, me. Wanna chat?"

"All right."

"You sound kinda new. Been doing this long?"

"First time."

"Nothing to be scared of. What's your name?"

"Andrew."

"Hi, Andrew. I'm Alex. Short for Alexandra."

"Hello, Alex."

"Wanna tell me about yourself?"

"What sort of thing?"

"Oh, what you do for a living, hobbies, sports, that kinda stuff."

"OK. Well, I'm an osteopath."

"That's bones, right?"

"That's right. I've just bought a house, so I'm spending a lot of time decorating. I go swimming once a week. What do you do?"

"I work for a film company. Sounds exciting, but I'm just an assistant. I play tennis, and we gotta pool at home."

"I've got a pond in the garden. It's frozen over now."

"Frozen over? Where the heck are you, Alaska?"

"Surrey."

"England? You're in England?"

"Yes. Where are you?"

"LA."

"Los Angeles?"

"Yep."

"But it must be nearly midnight over there!"

"My Mom lets me stay up late now I'm thirty. My Mom's English. I was raised over here, but I've been to England a coupla times. You been out here?"

"I'd like to."

"Broke, huh?"

"It's not that. It'll sound stupid."

"I won't laugh."

"I'm afraid of flying."

"What - you've never been on a plane?"

"Once. Never again."

"How d'you get back, then?"

"Train. Luckily it was only Glasgow."

"You gonna have therapy for it or something?"

"No. I think everyone has their Achilles' heel. This is mine. I can live with it."

"That's cool. You got any brothers or sisters?"

"One brother. He's married."

"He older than you?"

"Yes. He's thirty-six, I'm thirty-four."

"Must be nice having a brother."

"We get on OK. Have you got any sisters?"

"Nah. Just me. Did I tell you my Dad's from New York? My Dad's from New York and my Mom's from England and we live in LA. No wonder I'm one mixed-up kid. So tell me what you look like."

"Oh. Well, I'm tall, dark-"

"Stop there. Let a girl dream. You gotta girlfriend?"

"Not at the moment."

"What sort of women do you like?"

"I'm not sure."

"You like cute? I can do cute. You like sassy? Sassy's a cinch."

"Tall, I suppose."

"I'm 5'11"."

"That is tall."

"In heels. 5'11" in heels. Blonde hair, blue eyes."

"Sounds great."

"You don't like blondes, huh? I can be brunette, too. Just give it a while for the color to wash out."

"I'm sure you're fine just the way you are."

"Hey, kid, you're nice, anyone ever tell you that?"

"I have my moments."

"My life is just one long moment. Guess I'll have to put it down to lousy hormones. Did I tell you I'm single? Pretty obvious, huh?"

Email between Alex and Andrew on Friday 28th August 1998:

"Hi, Andrew. How ya doing?"

"Fine. And you?"

"Great. Big party this weekend."

"Have fun."

"I will. What you got planned?"

"Mowing the lawn, catching up with some paperwork. Oh, and we're going out for a meal. Just my brother and his wife, and one of their friends."

"Male or female?"

"Female."

"They setting you up, your brother and his wife?"

"I don't think so."

"Think again, kid. So what, you're thirty-four?"

"Thirty-five."

"Hey, I missed your birthday! Must have been a big cake, all those candles."

"Enormous."

"Thirty-five. Single. Eligible. Nice house, good job - any girl would jump at the chance."

"Not everyone's so materialistic. Anyway, I thought you said you had a tennis court and a pool at home."

"Oh, I meant my Mom and Dad's house. I'm starving in an attic."

"People must be interested when you tell them you're in the film industry."

"Hell, everyone's in the movie industry. There are so many movie producers, the furniture stores sell casting couches!"

Email between Alex and Andrew on Saturday 12th September 1998:

"You there, Alex?"

"What? Oh, hi, Andrew."

"You sound distracted."

"Gotta tidy the place."

"Someone coming?"

"Yeah."

"Anyone special?"

"I guess."

"OK, I'll let you get on with it."

"Sorry, kid. Another time."

"Let me know how it goes."

"I can tell you that now."

"Come on, Alex, it'll be all right."

"Yeah, yeah, look on the bright side and all that crap."

"You're sure you're in the mood for this?"

"Oh, yes! I've already found a sneaker under the bed. I thought I'd lost it."

"I'm not talking about the spring-cleaning."

"I know. Yeah, you're right. Maybe Mr Right'll walk through the door tonight."

"One day it'll happen."

"Who needs men, anyway?"

"Thanks, Alex."

"Oh, you know I didn't mean you. Who am I trying to kid, anyhow? I wouldn't be cleaning up if it didn't matter."

"Take a break."

"Maybe I will. Gotta go out anyway and get some wine. Maybe some flowers, too. Brighten the place up."

"Well, have a nice evening."

"Yeah, maybe I just will. Thanks, kid."

Email between Alex and Andrew on Saturday 21st November 1998:

"You wanna talk dirty?"

Pause.

"Alex, I'm having my breakfast!"

"Shit. I keep forgetting the time difference. While I'm some misfit with no place to go tonight, you're up and about and bursting with energy. Are you bursting with energy?"

"Let me finish my coffee first. Or have you started talking dirty?"

"You'll have to figure that one out by yourself. Wanna know what I'm wearing?"

"Is it hot?"

"It's so hot, it's cool! Oh, the weather. You're just like my Mom. Why do you English always insist on talking about the weather?"

"Because it rules our lives. Will I need my umbrella today? Will I have to scrape the ice off the windscreen? Should I wear a scarf?"

"Are you wearing a scarf?"

"No, just my pyjamas?"

"Hey, you know how to turn a girl on after all. Are they silk? Do they caress your skin?"

"No, they're just ordinary Marks and Spencer's brushed cotton pyjamas."

"Forget about you. Guess what I'm wearing."

"A bin bag and bed socks."

"You peeked! Have another guess."

"Thermal long johns and a tutu."

"Is this your British sense of humor, or should I be getting seriously worried that you're some kinda nut?"

"OK. What are you wearing?"

"You could show some enthusiasm. I put them on specially for you."

Another pause.

"Look, Alex-"

"Yeah, I know. Come on, it'll be fun. Loosen up. Lose some of those inhibitions."

"I thought you'd understand - you're half English."

"Not the half I'm thinking about. You want me to tell you?"

A pause.

"OK."

"Nylons, one of those things to keep them up - I don't know what you English call them - and a man's shirt."

"Sounds fairly respectable."

"Now guess what I'm not wearing."

"Ah."

"You got it! Panties! Knickers. I'm not wearing any knickers."

"Oh."

"Wanna see? Damn, no video link. I guess I'll just have to describe it. You tell me about yours, I'll tell you about mine."

"Alex, I've never done this before."

"You've never had cyber sex? You mean I've found myself a cyber virgin at last? Wow - virginal reality, man!"

"Try holding on to the reality aspect, Alex."

"I'm unbuttoning my shirt. Want me to start at the top?"

"OK, you win."

"Hey, I need the audience on my side. A little enthusiasm would help. This isn't easy, you know. That's cheating! You got your eyes closed."

"Don't worry, my imagination's working overtime."

"That's more like it! I'm on the last button now. Wanna open your eyes? Here's Alex!"

"Nice."

"Is that all you can say?"

"We British are very restrained."

"What about this, then?"

"What are you doing?"

"Ah, that's got you interested. I'm taking my shirt off. Now I'm turning my chair round and sitting astride it. Liza Minnelli eat your heart out!"

A pause.

"Are you still there, Alex?"

"Yeah. Give me a minute."

Another pause.

"Drat."

"What's wrong?"

"Sally Bowles can't have used a computer in her act."

"Leave the mouse alone, Alex."

"Hey, what sort of pervert do you think I am? Mind you, the joystick might be worth investigating. I was turning the chair back, if you must know."

"Problems?"

"Couldn't reach the keyboard."

"Are you sure you've done this before?"

"Not with someone as uptight as you. Are you up tight?"

"Not yet."

"You're meant to lie."

"Are you lying?"

"Wouldn't know the truth if I fell over it. You're making it very hard."

"Thought that was the idea."

"Are we into role-swapping here? D'you wanna have the nylons?"

"I wouldn't want to deprive you of the sheer pleasure of wearing them."

"I'll take them off, if you like. I've got very long legs."

"You'd better hurry."

"Ah, sounds like we're getting somewhere. Maybe a shade premature, but we can work on that some other time."

"Alex, I need a shave!"

"I like stubble. Hey, can I have the shaver first? Only I forgot to do my legs."

"I really have to go."

"But you haven't come yet! Or did I miss something?"

"Damn! Now I'm all sticky."

"Eureka!"

"Hardly. I've just put my elbow in the marmalade."

"Marmalade, hmm? Could be interesting. Is it the smooth stuff, or is it the stuff with bits in?"

"Oh, Alex, go out and find someone nice."

"The nice ones are married. Hey, you're not married, are you?"

"No, I'm not married."

"Something wrong with you?"

"I'm a touch mad."

"What's got you mad?"

"What? Oh, I see. No, not mad angry. Mad insane. Even to be talking to you."

"Look on it as your good deed for the day. And, believe me, it's very, very good."

"Alex, are you talking dirty again?"

"Don't interrupt a girl when she's busy."

Pause.

"I know, I know. But don't knock it until you've tried it. You still there?"

"Yes."

"You mad at me? Mad angry, I mean."

"No."

"Thanks, kid."

"What for?"

"For being there. Shit, my Mom's coming over tomorrow and the keys are all sticky! I'd better wipe them."

"Don't electrocute yourself."

"Hey, could I do that? Seriously?"

"I don't know."

"What if I unplugged the keyboard?"

"Would the computer go down on you?"

"I don't know, I'll have to ask it. It's about the only hope I've got these days. And don't say, 'Oh, Alex!' again in that tone of voice."

"Go to bed!"

"I love macho men!"

"Idiot. Look, I've really got to go. Are you all right?"

"Talk to me again?"

"Yeah."

"Your turn next time."

"What?"

"To talk dirty. Oh, don't look so worried. Just tip out the garbage can and tell me what's there."

"Sorry, Alex, I just can't-"

"I know. D'you mind if I do?"

"Did it help?"

"Not much. I kept thinking about toast and cereal. I suppose I shouldn't have tried to get laid on an empty stomach."

"Look after yourself."

"I do. D'you think they should classify cyber sex as safer sex?"

"Depends what you're doing!"

"Kid?"

"Yes?"

A pause.

"Nothing. Cheerio, old bean."

"Where do you get these expressions?"

Email then telephone conversation between Alex and Andrew on Wednesday 13th January 1999:

"Where've you been, Alex? You haven't spoken to me for at least a week."

"My best friend died."

"Oh, God! I'm sorry, Alex. Do you want to talk?"

"Not really. Just wanted to say 'hi'. Let you know I'm still here. Anyway. Better go now. Things to do. Sorry."

"Alex, don't go! Are you all right?"

"I'm here, aren't I?"

"You know what I mean."

"Do I? I don't know anything any longer. Talk to you next week."

"Don't go! I'll give you my phone number. Talk to me NOW!"

"Don't shout, I can't bear it."

"Sorry. Here's my number."

Andrew gives Alex his number.

"I can't talk to you. You're the one person I can't talk to."

"I know, Alex. Did you think I didn't know? It's all right, I understand. That's why I'm worried about you."

"So that's your phone number, huh?"

"Yes. Please ring me."

Pause. Phone rings. Andrew picks up receiver.

"Alex? Is that you?"

Pause.

"I guess it must be."

"I'm sorry about your friend."

"Thanks."

"I think I know how he died. That's why I'm so worried."

"Don't be. I'm fine. I'll survive."

"Was ... he your partner?"

"No, we were just close. Best friends. Never went to bed with each other. Probably why we stayed friends. Sorry I let you think I was female."

"I had my suspicions from the start."

"Pretty lousy woman, huh?"

"But a pretty nice man."

"You ever read Armistead Maupin?"

"Who? Oh, no. Why?"

"Doesn't matter."

"Can I do anything? Can I help?"

"I thought you'd want to beat the crap out of me for trying to talk dirty to you."

"Forget it. It was nothing."

"Nah, we didn't really get it on, did we? My gay friends get ill, so now I hit on straight guys."

"Alex, don't. Is that your real name?"

"Yeah. I suppose you're used to dealing with nuts, what with you being a doctor."

"I'm an osteopath."

"Whatever. Maybe I should go see a shrink."

"Alex, you're not a nut!"

"So picking up straight guys on the internet is normal behavior?"

"You were just lonely. Were there others?"

"Jealous, huh? No, not really. I stuck with you. You sounded nice. Besides, you were a coupla thousand miles away. I felt safe. I can't figure out why you've been talking to me, though."

"At the beginning maybe it was just a game. Trying not to give away the fact that I knew you were a man. Waiting for you to own up."

"Game over. You won."

"It stopped being a game a long time ago. Let me help. There must be something I can do."

"Keep on answering my emails?"

"Sure. Anything else?"

"Tell me sometime who the hell Dale Winton is."

"OK."

"What's the weather like?"

"Quite nice. It's stopped raining."

"Is that a joke?"

"It wasn't meant to be. Look, I'm going to my parents' house this weekend. I'll give you their number. I'll let you have my work number, too, just in case."

"Pretty soon you'll be giving me the number of your orthodontist."

"I don't have - OK, I get the message. But promise me you'll phone if you need to."

"OK. What'll you tell your folks? 'Hey, Mom, if this gay guy calls, I wanna speak with him'?"

"Maybe I'll just say one of my patients needs counselling."

"Long distance???"

"It's a friend."

"You'll have me crying again. So we're friends?"

"Yes."

"You wanna drop by for meat loaf sometime?"

"If I'm in the neighbourhood."

"It's late. I'd better hang up."

"Will you be all right?"

"I guess so. Thanks, kid."

"I'm glad you phoned."

"Tootle pip!"

"Bye."

Telephone conversation between Alex and Andrew on Monday 12th April 1999:

"I read that book you told me about."

"Yeah? Which one was that?"

"The one by Armistead Maupin. By the way, how did he get a name like that?"

"Just lucky, I guess. What did you think of it?"

"I liked it. So did my mother."

"You lent Tales of the City to your Mom? That's like coming out to her."

"She knows I'm straight."

"Are you sure?"

"I should know."

"The lady doth protest too much, methinks."

Telephone conversation between Alex and Andrew on Sunday 21st November 1999:

"Guess what?"

"They're sending a manned space mission to Mars, and they've asked you to go."

"Close. I'm coming to Britain next month. I guess they figured I could speak the language."

"London?"

"No, Edinburgh."

"Just down the road, really."

"Wanna meet up? I could stop off in London for the day. We could do something."

"Sounds fine. A pity you can only stay one day. I could have shown you around properly."

Pause.

"Well, I could stay longer. I just thought you wouldn't be able to take my company for more than twenty-four hours."

"Idiot! When are you coming?"

"January 8. I've got some things to do in Edinburgh. Work stuff. Shouldn't take more than a week."

"OK. Let me check what I'm doing. I'll phone you back. D'you want to stay with me?"

Pause.

"It was just a thought."

"It's just ... well, I'm this weirdo from LA who you've never met, and you don't seem to mind."

"You haven't met me, either."

"What - you're telling me you got some awful secret? I mean like you're a stamp collector or something?"

"I grind my teeth in my sleep."

"Maybe I'll be there one day when you do. You want me to bring anything when I come? You know, popcorn, Coke, that kinda thing?"

"No, it'd only cause a riot. People here aren't used to such luxuries."

Face-to-face on Saturday 15th January 2000, Heathrow, 11.15am.:

"Thought you'd look like some computer nerd."

"Thought you'd be some camp queen."

Alex and Andrew smile at each other.

"Well, I'm here."

"If the mountain won't go ... "

"You are kinda tall, I guess."

"Only 6'3"."

"Only 6'3", huh? What am I, some kind of dwarf?"

"My brother is 6'6"."

"What is it, something they're putting in the water?"

"My Dad's tall. Even my mother's 6'."

"Sheesh, your Mom's taller than me? Musta been great when you were at school. Other kids boasted that their Dad was bigger than your Dad. You boasted that your Mom was bigger than their Dad."

"Sorry you had to come here."

"Gee, thanks. I've only been here five minutes."

"No, I meant I'm sorry it couldn't have been me going out to California."

"You freaking out here?"

"What, the airport, you mean? Oh, no, airports don't bother me. As long as I don't have a plane ticket. Do you want a coffee before we go home?"

"No. Hey, you sure it's alright for me to stay? I could check into some hotel if you like."

"Don't be stupid. Of course it's all right. I wouldn't have invited you if it wasn't."

"Maybe I should call my Mom. I've never been on a sleepover before. Do we stay up late and talk about boys?"

"It's not obligatory."

"Gee, you know all these long words ..."

"How was the flight from Edinburgh?"

"Too short. Guess I'll have to join the mile-high club some other time. Hey, why are none of your place names pronounced the way they're written?"

"It's just to confuse foreigners. We took down signposts during the war for the same reason."

"Did it confuse the enemy?"

"Shouldn't think so, but it baffled some of us, so I understand."

"So we're off to Effingham?"

"If you ask a taxi driver for effing Ham, you'll be taken to a little place near Richmond."

"Gee, you have a Richmond over here, too?"

"When is it you go back to the States?"

"So, tell me what you got planned for us."

"Well, we could do the whole tourist thing. St Paul's, The Tower of London, Buckingham Palace, the museums."

"I've done most of them with my Mom. Still, I guess it would be kinda fun to see them again."

"There's the Dome, now. You queue for a couple of hours, and then they frisk you."

"All the inconveniences of modern air travel without going anyplace. Sounds fun. You'd enjoy it."

"Or there's the Scene."

"The Scene?"

"The Gay Scene. I bought a magazine ... It tells you where to go."

"Is this 'you' as in me, Alex, or 'you' as in we?"

"I suppose as I'm your host ..."

"What would you like to do? A few days off, how would you spend them?"

"Well, the hall needs decorating ..."

"Gee, you sure know how to show a guy a good time."

"Bath. It's a place."

"Yeah. Roman. Spas. Jane Austen. Anywhere else?"

"Paris. Bruges. Amsterdam."

"Did somebody move them when I wasn't looking? I coulda sworn they were in France or someplace like that. How d'you get there – swim the Channel?"

"Ferry. The Channel Tunnel. Paris is closer than Edinburgh."

"Weird continent you got here. Kinda cute, though."

"Gee, thanks."

Face-to-face on Saturday 22nd January 2000:

"Can I ask a question?"

"You just did."

"Did you really have stockings on?"

"Nah. I was just making it up. Another one of my fantasies. Like having sex with this straight guy I know. You got any fantasies?"

"None I'm prepared to tell you."

"Spoilsport."

"Come on, I've got a surprise for you."

They go next door.

"You gotta couch in here! Or do you call it a bed or a table or something?"

"Never mind what it's called."

"Are we gonna do what I hope we're gonna do?"

"I thought you might like a massage."

"Nice thought, but no thanks. I know what would happen as soon as you laid a finger on me, and it would embarrass the hell out of both of us. The National Lottery's on TV soon. I thought I'd give it a whirl."

"It wouldn't embarrass me."

Pause.

"You mean you'd ...? You'd really ...?"

"Yes. You're forgetting I'm an osteopath."

"So?"

"I work with my hands."

Pause while implication sinks in.

"Guess I'll just have to catch up with old Dale some other time."

Telephone conversation between Alex and Andrew on Sunday 30th January 2000:

"Hi, Alex."

"Hello, Andrew. You OK? You want me to send you a spoon or something?"

"A spoon?"

"Yeah. You know what they say about supping with the devil ..."

"No, I'm fine."

"Thanks. I didn't expect ... It was nice. Maybe I could reciprocate sometime."

"Maybe."

"Anyway, what's been happening?"

Telephone conversation between Alex and Andrew on Sunday 6th February 2000:

"So Section 28 is being repealed, huh?"

"It's not as easy as that. It's still got to go before the House of Lords."

"I thought they'd been abolished or something."

"Or something. I think there's meant to be a free vote."

"Huh?"

"No whips."

"So that's what they mean by sexual politics. I always wondered."

"I'll tell you about private member's bills another time, shall I?"

"Yeah. Too much excitement's bad for me."

Telephone conversation between Alex and Andrew on Sunday 13th February 2000:

"And they actually called it that? Domosexual Day?"

"It was in the papers."

"So it must have been true."

"And the age of consent's been reduced to sixteen."

"You mean we got equality?"

"That's right. You can even join the Armed Forces – that happened a couple of weeks ago, but I kept forgetting to tell you."

"What's with the sudden interest in gay politics?"

"Just thought I'd keep you up to date."

"If I didn't know any better ..."

Email then telephone conversation between Alex and Andrew on Saturday 10th June 2000:

"Why are we communicating by email again? Aren't you speaking to me?"

Pause.

"I think I'm coming down with a cold."

"Wanna hear a joke?"

"Alex – "

"It's a good joke."

"Alex, please listen."

"You're the one not talking to me."

"I went out last night."

"You see, this guy goes to a movie."

"With a girl."

"And you slept with her."

"Yes."

"How was it?"

"OK."

"Only OK?"

"Yes. I'm sorry."

"Sorry that it was only OK?"

"Alex, don't."

"So how d'you feel today?"

"Guilty as hell."

"Hey, I'm the Pope, I absolve you."

"I didn't even know you were Catholic."

"I'm not. Anyway, it doesn't count with girls."

Pause.

"Kid, are you still there?"

"I miss you."

"You sound kinda funny."

"Sorry."

"Are you crying?"

"Yes."

"Hell, don't electrocute yourself!"

"We've used that gag before."

"Hey, it's alright. I'm not going to come over there and beat your brains out. So you messed up. Big deal."

"Anyway, I just thought you ought to know."

Andrew's phone is ringing.

"Pick up the phone, you dumb prick!"

"Is that you?"

"No, it's divine retribution calling. Pick up your God-damn phone!"

Andrew picks up the phone but says nothing.

"What's wrong, kid? Straight guys sleep with girls. It's just one of those things."

"But it wasn't what I wanted."

"What did you want?"

"I don't know. I keep thinking about you and me. Except there is no you and me. There's a whole continent between us and I can't even come over and see you because of my fear of flying. It's

not as if I can promise you anything. I don't want to give up my job, I don't want to leave my friends, and as for sex ..."

"Let me worry about that. You've told me what you don't want. What do you want?"

"To see you. I want to see you. But I feel stupid and weak and guilty."

"Quit with the self-flagellation."

"Sorry."

"You ever see Notting Hill?"

"She's American and he's English?"

"That, too. The crummy scene where he say's he's just this guy ... They say it twice just in case you missed it first time round."

"I don't remember."

"Never mind. Want me to come over?"

"What, to England?"

"I know you're not one of the major league players any more, but a few intrepid pilots still drop food parcels, don't they? Maybe I could parachute in with some chocolate or something."

"I'll send you the airfare."

"I don't take hand-outs. I'll charge it to my Dad's account. He'll never notice."

Face-to-face on Tuesday 27th June 2000:

At Andrew's house. Andrew and Alex hug each other. Andrew is aroused.

"Hey, you want a massage?"

"Sorry."

"I'm the one should be sorry. I'm too tired. Can't figure out whether it's today or tomorrow. Where am I sleeping?"

"Wherever you want."

"Where do you want me to sleep?"

"With me. I want you to sleep with me."

"OK."

"Alex?"

"What?"

"Oh, nothing. I mean I'm glad you're here."

Later same day:

"Hi."

"Hello. Good sleep?"

"Yeah."

"Hungry?"

"Not really. A coffee would be nice. What were you gonna say? Just before I hit the sack?"

"Nothing important."

Pause.

"I come God knows how many thousand miles for you to clam up on me?"

"It's not easy, Alex. In fact, it scares the hell out of me."

"It's beginning to scare the shit out of me. You getting married or something?"

"No."

"Come on. I won't give you a hard time, whatever it is."

"I like talking to you. I like being with you. I liked it when I ... And I've missed you. I think it might be love."

"I could use that cup of coffee now."

"What? Oh, yes, of course. I'll get you one."

Goes to kitchen, returns with coffee.

"Of course, it would never have worked. I don't know if you could have got a job over here. I don't even know if you could have stayed. Just forget I said anything. We'll do the sights, shall we? You know, I've never been inside Buckingham Palace. Perhaps now would be ..."

"Quiet! I'm trying to think."

"Sorry."

"Just for the record, I love you, too. It's my Mom that's the problem. Having to tell her there's this English guy I've fallen for."

"I thought she knew you were gay?"

"Hell, she's known that for years. No, it's that you're English. Well, not really that, either. More that you're here. In England. Since that last bust-up with – well, never mind, she's sworn she'll never set foot over here. And you can't come to the States. How the hell are you two ever gonna meet each other?"

"Paris?"

"Paris? Hey, she likes Paris. Kid, you're a genius."

"But what are we going to do?"

"Well, I'm gonna get a refund on my airline ticket."

"But you can't just stay. You'd probably end up an illegal immigrant. They'd deport you. It'd be a nightmare."

"Relax, kid. It'll be alright."

"All right? Even if I could just hop on a plane to America, it'd just be swapping one set of problems for another. We need to find out where we stand. We've got to do this by the book. Legally."

"Trust me, Andrew, everything'll be fine."

"How can you say that? I don't want to be looking over my shoulder all the time. Alex, it's not all right, it's a mess!"

"Gee, you really are worked up about this, aren't you?"

"I'm sorry. I just don't want to lose you."

"There's really nothing to worry about."

"Oh, Alex …"

"No, I mean it, kid. There is absolutely nothing to worry about. Maybe I should have told you before. I thought it might scare you off."

"Told me what?"

"Where's my bag? Ah, here it is. I've got something to show you."

Produces passport.

"I don't understand."

"No, that's not it."

Alex rummages in bag again and brings out something else.

"Ta-ra!"

"What's that?"

"What does it look like?"

"But how ...?"

"My Mom and me came out to the States when I was three. My step-Dad's American. My real Dad is English."

"You mean, after all you've said, you're really one of us?"

"Gee, and I thought I was one of them! Ouch, that hurt!"

"You let me think you were American when all the time ..."

"I guess it must have slipped my mind. Anyway, I am American. Stop doing that!"

"You did it on purpose, you ... hypocrite!"

"Hypocrite? Forget hypocrite. What about the Hippocratic oath? Get off me!"

"First you pretend to be a woman-"

"Don't do that! You know I'm sensitive there!"

"Then this! Is there anything else I should know?"

"No! Honestly. This is it. Don't worry about my Mom, she'll come round. Literally. She never stays mad with my real Dad for long."

"Oh, Alex, what am I going to do with you!"

"I can think of a few things."

"You've got a one-track mind!"

"Maybe I do. But that's not all I got." Alex waves a second passport at Andrew. "I got dual nationality."

****

THE COLD LIGHT OF DAY

"Are you all right?"

"What?"

"You look very pale. Are you sure you're all right?"

"Yes. Yes, I'm fine," said Jamie unconvincingly.

"Let me get you a glass of water. It's been a long day for everyone."

Jamie nodded, glad to allow someone else to take charge.

It didn't take long for Paul to fetch the water. "Here you are," he said, holding out the glass.

Jamie looked at it blankly.

"Come on, come and sit down." Paul shepherded him into a side room where there were a couple of chairs. "Too many buck's fizzes?" he suggested lightly. Jamie didn't look drunk to him, more shell-shocked, but at least he had now sat down and was sipping the water.

"Thanks." A forlorn smile, but a smile nevertheless.

"It's been a stressful day," Paul said.

Jamie nodded.

"You did very well. The speech was brilliant."

"It wasn't what I wanted to say."

"Well, maybe one day you'll get the chance to say the rest."

"Things'll be different now."

Paul looked searchingly at Jamie. "You've known Daniel a long time, haven't you?"

Jamie nodded again. "Since primary school."

"And today he got married," Paul said quietly.

Jamie stared unseeingly in front of him.

"Shall I take the glass?"

Jamie seemed not to understand, so Paul repeated his question.

"Oh, yes. Sorry." Jamie returned the empty glass, but, instead of taking it back to the dining-room, Paul gazed thoughtfully at Jamie.

"You look whacked out. Let me give you a lift home," he said.

"I can't go home," Jamie said simply.

"They can manage without you. After all, you didn't lose the rings, you remembered your speech, and you've seen the bride and groom off on their honeymoon. Come on, there's nothing more you can do."

"The presents …" Jamie began.

"Louise's sister's taken charge of the presents."

"I should say goodbye. I shouldn't just leave."

"I'll tell them you're not feeling well. They'll understand."

"I can't go home," Jamie said again. "I just …" He broke off. How could he explain that the thought of being by himself terrified him?

"Come back with me, then," Paul said.

Jamie looked up sharply. Of course, he'd heard the rumours, but had never paid much attention to them. Why wasn't Paul married? people asked. He must be in his mid-thirties, and no one had seen him with a girl. Someone claimed that Paul and another man had shared a flat in the same block as a friend of his, but it all sounded a bit tenuous.

"Just for a cup of coffee," said Paul, as if aware of Jamie's thoughts. "And a talk. You look as if you need to talk."

Jamie hesitated, but then nodded. "Yes, you're right. I've got to tell someone."

And so they'd gone back to Paul's flat.

Jamie stared at the magazine on the coffee table, then glanced up at Paul.

"I wasn't expecting visitors," said Paul, deftly removing a copy of Gay Times and putting it on the rack underneath.

"Sorry," Jamie said.

"It's all right. Saves an explanation. What can I get you? Tea, coffee – or something stronger?"

"I don't mind." In his present state, even deciding what to drink seemed too much.

"OK. Well, sit down. I won't be long." Paul smiled, then disappeared into the kitchen.

Jamie did as he was told. He wondered what he was doing there in Paul's flat.

Paul was soon back, carrying two mugs of coffee.

"Thanks," said Jamie, surprised that Paul hadn't given him an alcoholic drink.

"I put sugar in yours. It's supposed to be good for shock. Have you eaten?"

"Not much. I wasn't hungry. All that food ..." He shrugged.

"I'll make us some cheese on toast in a minute."

"I'm not sure that I can eat anything. I'm just so tired," said Jamie.

"Have something to eat. Or does cheese give you nightmares?"

"I wouldn't mind if it did. I don't dream now. I haven't been sleeping well. And, even if I do nod off, I find that no sooner have I done so than it's time to get up again."

"Perhaps if you tell me what's wrong, you'll find your insomnia disappears."

"It was having to write the speech that did it," Jamie was saying. "For weeks I'd tried to put it off, found excuses not to do it. Then my mother wanted to hear it. 'Only a month now,' she'd said. So I started. And instead of saying how happy I hoped Danny and Louise would be, I was saying how miserable I'd be.

"Me and Danny, it had always been me and Danny. And gradually I began to glimpse other things, things I'd only half-acknowledged before. And still I couldn't really believe it, couldn't accept it. I was letting my imagination run away with me, that was all it was. Danny was my best friend, always had been, it was as simple as that. So why was it so painful?

"Eventually I understood I was grieving. Everything we'd shared together was over. Danny had grown up and moved on, but I hadn't. I just wanted things to remain the same. I didn't want to lose him. I loved him.

"I loved him. I sat there for ages thinking that. Everything fell into place. How I felt when I was with him, my sense of loss when he said he and Louise were getting married, the strange dreams I used to have before I stopped dreaming altogether. I don't know what happens now. I suppose I have to learn to live with the fact that Danny and Louise are married, but I don't know what I do about my newfound sexuality. It was so easy with Danny around, I didn't have to do anything. My whole social life revolved around Danny. What he did, I did. What do I do now – wear an AIDS ribbon? Take out a subscription to Gay Times? See if there's a local gay society? It all seems to require so much effort, and I'm tired. I dream of lying on a beach somewhere with nothing to do, no thoughts going round in my head, and sleeping for ten hours. Maybe that's all I need: a holiday. But even the idea of having to book one puts me off. I don't want to do anything, I can't. I just want someone else to tell me what to do, to tell me it's all right, to say I'll get through this.

"And the one person I want to tell, I can't. It would spoil everything. If Danny knew how I felt about him, he'd feel sorry for me, and I don't want his pity.

"So there you are. That's all it was – a twist on the conventional love triangle, only I didn't realise how I felt until Danny and Louise got engaged. Pretty stupid, huh? But not half as stupid as failing to see that I was gay. That's unbelievable."

For a long while, they sat in silence.

"You just fell in love with the wrong person," said Paul quietly. "It can happen to anyone. It's not stupid. And a lot of people find it hard to accept they're gay. It means coming to terms with a new reality. A straight person is expected to be straight. He doesn't agonise over whether to tell anyone, he doesn't need to. It's simple.

"At the moment, forget about being gay – it's irrelevant. You've just lost someone close to you, and you're right, you are grieving. I think you may be depressed, too. Not just upset, but clinically depressed, if that's what it's called. You'd feel awful enough suffering from insomnia even without everything else that's happened lately. I think you should go and see your doctor, see what they recommend. They might prescribe something short-term to help restore your sleep patterns, or they might suggest you need to talk to someone. A professional, someone who knows what to do in these circumstances. Maybe I'm wrong, maybe being gay is part and parcel of it all, I don't know." Paul stopped and smiled, embarrassed. "Sorry. I didn't intend making a speech. You've probably had enough of those today."

"No, what you said makes sense. I need to …" He searched for the right words. "Let go."

"Well, anytime you want to talk ..." said Paul.

Jamie knew it was his cue to leave. He stood up.

"Will you be all right?" Paul asked.

Jamie nodded, but avoided eye contact.

Paul saw Jamie's pale, drawn face, his slumped shoulders, and general air of defeat. Deep within him a memory stirred and then rose on fragile, gossamer wings which beat softly but steadily.

"You could stay here. I could make up a bed on the sofa." When Jamie didn't reject his suggestion, Paul went to find some bedclothes. He came back carrying a duvet and a pillow. "Here."

Jamie looked up, and for a few seconds they stared into each other's eyes. Jamie swallowed. "I just want to be with someone. Not sex, I didn't mean ..." His voiced trailed off. "I'm sorry. The sofa's fine."

"Come on," said Paul gently, putting the duvet and pillow down. "You can share my bed."

Paul grinned as Jamie got into bed beside him. "You'll be lucky to get any sleep tonight," he said, in an effort to cheer Jamie up.

Jamie managed a tired smile. "Why's that?"

"I snore like a wart-hog with a bad cold."

Again they stared at each other. Two adults sharing a bed, each sexually aware of the other.

"Good night," said Paul softly.

"Hi."

"Hello," said Paul. "Did you manage to get some sleep?"

"Yes. I only woke up ten minutes ago."

"So my snoring didn't keep you awake, then?"

"I didn't notice it. I slept like a log for the first time in weeks. I actually feel human today."

"I'm glad," Paul said, genuinely pleased for Jamie.

"Thanks." Jamie leant across meaning simply to kiss Paul lightly on the cheek, but then the unforgivable happened – he got an erection. "Sorry," he said, moving quickly away.

"Our bodies let us down sometimes," said Paul understandingly. He hesitated, then added, "Mind you, it usually pays to listen to what they're telling us."

Jamie sat up, unsure. This was unfamiliar territory. “It would feel like I was just using you,” he said eventually.

“Most people would see it differently. They’d say I was trying to seduce you because you’re young and vulnerable.”

“Then they’d be wrong,” Jamie said quietly. He stared in front of him while he made up his mind. “Does it hurt?” he asked at last.

It hadn’t hurt, well, not what they’d done, anyway. So what if he hadn’t exactly lost his virginity? There’d been comfort and tenderness and he’d taken the first step along the road that was his future.

Just as they were leaving, Jamie put his hand on Paul’s arm before he could open the front door. “Thanks,” he said, and smiled. “For everything.”

“That’s all right. We all need someone to talk to from time to time.”

“Can I ask you something?”

Paul nodded.

“Have you … has there never been anyone special?” Jamie said awkwardly, wondering if his question would be seen as an unwarranted intrusion.

“There was once,” Paul said briefly. He shrugged. “It just didn’t work out. Come on, I’ll drive you back to the hotel so you can pick up your car.”

Paul glanced down at his hands resting on the steering wheel. Even in the cold light of day, the scars on his wrist were hardly visible.

****

BROTHERLY LOVE

"It'll never work!"

"It's worth a try. I've got to get my own back somehow after that trick he played on me a few months ago. All we've got to do is cross out a couple of words."

"I don't know how you managed to get him to fall for it anyway. A lonely hearts column!"

"I said he didn't have the nerve to do it. Besides, he'll be thirty this year. Practically senile."

"You won't get away with it. He'll never go on an actual date."

"That doesn't matter. Just think of his face when he sees the replies!"

"But trying to set him up with another man ... He's your brother, after all."

"That didn't stop him, did it? This is how it reads at the moment. 'Nice guy, late twenties, friendly, honest, easy-going, straight, looking for long term relationship would like to meet similar female.' Now all I have to do is change a few things et voila! 'Nice guy, etc, etc, straight-looking would like to meet similar for long term relationship.' What d'you think?"

"He'll never speak to you again!"

Why on earth had he let his brother talk him into putting an ad in the paper? Peter asked himself as he cleaned the car the following weekend. Heaven knew what kind of response it would get. Why didn't he just go to The Pyramid and hope to meet someone there?

He threw the sponge into the bucket and sighed. He'd been going to The Pyramid on a Saturday night for the past five years and where had it got him? There'd been a few girls, of course, but nothing that had lasted. He'd be thirty soon, and what had he to show for it? A house that had been invaded by his brother and his dozy friend; a car that went with the job; and a computer that was obsolete before it left the shop. He wasn't sure, but he thought he might even be losing his hair.

Peter paused for a minute. All around were the bright yellows, dry browns and occasional fiery red of an English autumn. The car was far better than he could have afforded himself, the computer more user-friendly than some state-of-the-art models he'd seen, and Ant and Luke were company in their own way. He didn't really have much to complain about, he thought. Just as long as that brother of his didn't tell anyone about the advertisement.

"Read this – it's amazing!"

"God, you're not going to show it to Pete, are you?"

"Why not? Here, you take that one while I have a look at this."

"This one sounds nice."

"This one sounds desperate – they'll make a great couple!"

" 'Fair hair, blue eyes … ' "

"He says he wants to act out his wildest fantasies."

" '5'7", I'm a nurse at the Royal.' I've always wanted to go out with a nurse."

"Well, you write back to him, then. What does 'tantric' mean?"

" 'I've never dared answer a lonely hearts before, but there was something about your ad that made me decide to write. Hope to hear from you soon, Chris.' Hell, Ant, he sounds nice."

"Fix him up with one of the others if you're so concerned. Now when shall we – What did you say?"

"He sounds nice."

"No, the last bit of the letter."

" 'Hope to hear from you soon, Chris.' "

"That's it! That's the one. We can throw the others away."

"But I thought …"

"Don't you see? The name. It'll never cross Pete's mind that it's from another man."

"You don't seriously mean ... You're not going to let Pete write back, are you?"

Peter looked around him. He'd never been in this pub before, and something struck him as odd. Then he realised that there were no women, only men, and that they were all looking at him. He wondered if his flies were undone.

Suddenly a hesitant voice said, "Peter?"

Peter whirled around. The person who had spoken was fair-haired, blue-eyed and carried a copy of the local newspaper. And, like the others, was male.

"Oh, my God!" said Peter.

"Vince," said the other man promptly.

"Oh, thank goodness for that. I thought you were … " Peter broke off.

"Queer as Folk."

"What?" Peter said, blankly.

"I'm Chris Turner. And you're straight." Anyone who hadn't heard of QAF couldn't possibly be gay. Chris smiled ruefully at Peter. "Looks like there's been a misunderstanding."

"You could say that!"

"Can I get you a drink? You look as if you need one. We could go somewhere else if you like. Another pub, I mean." Chris stood there, uncertain.

Peter took one look at his companion's open, honest face, and relaxed. "Yes, a drink would be nice. Here's fine," he added.

"Sorry about the mix-up. I don't know what could have happened."

"Oh, I expect it's my fault. I probably misread the ad. I don't know how, though – I must have read it a hundred times."

They bought a couple of drinks, and took them over to an empty table.

"Did you get many replies?" Chris asked, as he sipped a Diet Coke.

"No, yours was the only one. Did you …" Peter stopped, embarrassed.

"Did I answer any others? No, just yours." They grinned at each other.

"Not much of a success rate for either of us."

They chatted for a while. Peter found himself at ease with Chris, who was both sociable and sympathetic.

"Well, I suppose I won't be needing this," said Chris, indicating the local paper.

"D'you mind if I have a look? I haven't seen the ad actually in print."

"Here you are. You can't miss it."

Peter turned to the lonely hearts section towards the end. He found his ad straight away as there was a circle round it. He read it, then frowned. "I didn't write this. I said 'similar female'." He passed the paper back to Chris.

"They must have missed it out by mistake. What about this bit?" said Chris, indicating the part that read 'straight-looking'.

"I didn't put that, either. I wrote, 'straight, looking for long term relationship,' I'm sure I did. The paper was thrown out otherwise I'd never have let it get this far."

"Oh, these things happen. A pity mine was the only reply. If you'd had any Steves or Daves asking to meet you, you'd soon have realised something was wrong."

"Yes," said Peter absently. There was something nagging at the back of his mind, something not quite right. Ever since he'd decided to place the ad, there'd been a number of odd little incidents. Taken separately, nothing to speak of; but taken together, a pattern began to emerge. "The stamp," he said suddenly, the last piece of the jigsaw falling into place. "The stamp wasn't franked."

"What d'you mean?"

"Your reply – Ant must have read it, then put it in a different envelope. He must have hidden the paper, too, so I wouldn't see it. He set me up, the sod!" Peter realised immediately what he'd said, and was horrified. "Sorry, I didn't mean …"

"It's OK. Who's Ant?"

"My brother."

"You're saying he deliberately changed what you wrote?"

"Yes. My brother and his friend. And I thought they were being helpful! Look, I'm really sorry about all of this. He was just trying to get his own back."

"What had you done to annoy him so much?"

Peter pulled a face. "I told him the clocks had gone back, instead of forwards. How was I to know he was going to set the video for the last episode of some obscure TV series? "

Chris grinned. "Don't worry on my account. It's been a long time since I had such an entertaining evening." He glanced at his watch, then got out a mobile phone. "I promised I'd give someone a ring," he explained.

"My sister," he said when he'd finished. "I said I'd let her know if I needed rescuing." He looked at Peter as if a thought had just struck him. "Would you like to come back for a coffee?"

"Are you trying to proposition me?"

"Don't tell me you've never been curious ..." Chris's eyes danced with mischief.

"Not that curious," Peter said firmly.

"Pity."

"Come on, what's all this about?"

Chris outlined his plan.

"It'll never work," said Peter. "Will it?"

"Who was that on the phone?"

"Pete."

"I bet he was furious!"

"No. Apparently when he got to the pub there was a message saying that Chris couldn't make it."

"So it's all off, is it?"

"Not if I have anything to do with it!"

"Men!" fumed the girl sitting on the sofa. She glared at Peter and Chris as if she held them personally responsible for all the world's ills. "For years they had secretaries to do their typing for them. Woe betide the poor women if they didn't set it out properly or they mis-spelt something. Then computers come along, and men have to do their own letters. So what happens? Men suddenly find it's not as easy as they thought, and they can't be bothered to make the effort to do it properly. It's not even called typing any longer – it's word processing. They've got to bolster their poor little egos somehow." She stopped, and her eyes narrowed. "I suppose you want me to clear off upstairs so you can have a snog on the sofa?" she demanded truculently.

"Perhaps now's not a good moment …" Peter began hesitantly.

"Nonsense," said Chris. "We'll ask her now while she's in a good mood."

Peter looked doubtfully at Chris. He hoped he was joking.

"Wow! She's gorgeous."

"Close your mouth before someone sticks a bread roll in it."

"I wonder if she's with anyone."

"Quiet, she'll hear."

"Turner? Ant, she just said her name was Turner!"

"Stop panicking. When I phoned, they told me they'd got two bookings tonight in the name of Turner. She must be the other one."

"Hey, if she's meeting a girlfriend, maybe we could offer to buy them a drink or something. How do I look?"

"Is that the only suit you've got?"

"Yeah. I've only worn it once before – that was at my sister's wedding."

"When did she get married, 1955?"

"It's not that bad, is it? I know the sleeves are a bit short ..."

"Everything's a bit short. Did you have to wear those socks?"

"I like these socks. So what do we do now?"

"Wait. The table's booked for eight-thirty, so Pete should be here soon."

"What if he recognises us?"

"Your own mother wouldn't recognise you."

"And this dye washes out?"

"Eventually."

"What d'you mean, eventually? You told me …"

"Shhh. No, it's all right, it's not him."

"I still don't see why I had to dye my hair. Why couldn't I be the one hiding behind a newspaper?"

"He'd be bound to recognise me. And, besides, one of us has to keep an eye on the restaurant."

"I still say he'll call the whole thing off once he finds out who his dinner date is."

"He's here! OK, this is it."

"Why's he talking to that girl, Ant?"

"It'll be all right. She'll tell him he's made a mistake."

"They're going into the restaurant."

"He'll realise it's the wrong Turner when Chris turns up."

"That's a good one."

"What are you on about now?"

"Turner ... turns up. Very good."

"Where on earth is he? He should be here by now. You don't suppose he's chickened out, do you?"

"Maybe he had to work. I wonder what they're going to eat."

"What?"

"The waiter's given them both menus. I've heard they do a nice boeuf en croute here. D'you think they do take-aways? Ant?"

"What now?"

"You see that man over there?"

"The one with the walking stick?"

"Yes, that's the one. He looks pretty old."

"Must be eighty if he's a day."

"He's having a meal here, too."

"Well, it is a restaurant, for heaven's sake! Now be quiet, and keep a lookout for Chris."

"No, you don't understand. He's just said his name is Turner."

"Are they still watching us?" asked Peter, after he'd given the menu back to the waiter.

"Yes. I don't think they can believe what's happening." She grinned at Peter. "It's a good job I've got the same colouring as my brother or his plan wouldn't have got off the ground."

"I still feel guilty about what happened."

"There's no need to worry," said Claire. "He's out on a date."

"Not another lonely hearts, surely?"

"Not this time. One of his patients kept saying Chris had got to meet her grandson – Chris thought she meant some little kid. Well, when he came to visit, her grandson turned out to be six feet tall, and Chris said there was a lot of body language going on between the two of them. Both of them were too tongue-tied to say anything, though, so grandma ended up arranging for them to go to the cinema together."

"I hope it works out for Chris."

"Me, too. Sorry about the other evening. You caught me after a bad day at work."

"Thank goodness for that! I had thought tonight might be a complete disaster."

"So it's not a complete disaster?" Claire teased.

"Not so far. Perhaps I should advertise in the lonely hearts column more often," Peter remarked, his face innocent.

"What do we do now, Ant?"

"I don't know, Luke. I just don't know."

"We could go to the Pizza Pazza."

"Yeah."

"Or that new place that's just opened – you know, Junk Food. I think it must be Chinese."

"Mmm."

"Or we could just go home. There's some cold baked beans in the fridge. Maybe Pete will bring that girl back. I'd like to meet her."

"Luke?"

"What?"

"Shut up."

"OK. Ant?"

"What is it this time?"

"Well, I've been wondering ... This lonely hearts thing. Pete ended up with that girl. Maybe it's not such a bad idea after all. I'd quite like a girlfriend – the last one I had was three years ago. I can't help thinking you cramp my style. Don't get me wrong – I'd still like to hang out with you sometimes. I wouldn't want you to think I'd abandoned you or anything. What d'you reckon, then?"

For a minute Ant was speechless. Then his eyes narrowed speculatively. "Lonely hearts, eh? I suppose it might work. In fact, I'll help you with the ad, if you like."

****

LAST TIME IN BRUGES

It had been a spur-of-the-moment thing, their decision to return to Bruges. They'd been there years before, and had heard that it hadn't changed much. For that, they were grateful; there was too much that had changed recently, or perhaps it was just that they were older and less resilient.

A second honeymoon, Patrick had called it, just in fun, but Roger didn't mind; it would be pleasant to get away for a few days. Early spring. Before the crowds, but – if they were lucky – reasonable weather, although nothing could ever be guaranteed in northern Europe. A chance to forget the daily slog and to concentrate on what was really important. Who could tell if they'd get another chance?

Roger came from Southampton, was 5'9", had blue eyes, and was now completely bald. Patrick was a couple of inches shorter, and had blue eyes – though his were a darker shade – curly brown hair, and a soft Irish accent. They'd met in London, where Roger was in his last year at university in the days long before student loans had been dreamt of. And Patrick was working for a bank when banks were still crying out for staff.

After a brief fling, they'd lost touch for a couple of years, but then met again at a party where they found that the mutual attraction was still there.

Eventually they'd moved in together.

Patrick drove to Dover; then they caught the ferry to Calais; and then, finally, they drove on to Bruges. As they crossed the Franco-Belgium border, they grinned at each other.

"Remember our first taste of Belgium?" asked Roger.

"Smell, more like," said Patrick. "What on earth had they put on those fields? No wonder it was so strong – you'd opened the window!"

"I was hot. Anyway, I kept it closed for the rest of the journey. Next exit," he added after a while.

Their hotel was a large, modern two-storey building owned by a big hotel chain and seemingly in the middle of nowhere. They'd hoped to book somewhere with a bit more character, but had left it too late. At least here there was no problem parking, and the receptionists were polite and incurious when they checked in to their double room.

Patrick played with the television remote control ("Hey, there's BBC1, BBC2 and ITV!"), while Roger investigated the bathroom. The tap was the sort where one lever controlled both the flow and the temperature of the water. It was tricky; Patrick, a left-hander, had never mastered the art. Roger smiled as he read a notice in French. "Come in here," he called.

Patrick joined him. "Rearm?" he said disbelievingly. "What is it – a hairdryer or a nuclear warhead?"

"Must have gained something in the translation."

"So what do we do now?" asked Patrick, grinning mischievously.

"It's only three o'clock! I thought you'd want to do some sight-seeing."

"OK. Sight-seeing and then sex!"

"I might be tired," Roger warned him. "I'm not as young as I used to be."

"Then we'd better go easy on the sight-seeing. We could pretend to be tourists. You know, go for a ride in a horse-drawn carriage or in a boat on the canals."

"We are tourists, Patrick!" But he knew what Patrick was trying to do, knew there was seriousness beneath what seemed sometimes like flippancy.

"No, we're not – we've been here before, don't forget. We're practically locals. I could tell you exactly how to get to that bridge we sat on where the woman took our photo."

"I was sure this was it," said Patrick, puzzled. He'd already led them to several bridges which, for one reason or another, had been discounted. "But I don't remember those steps going down to the water."

"It'll do me," Roger said, hoping Patrick would be satisfied. "Anyway, you can't see if there are steps in the photo."

"I suppose not," Patrick conceded. He'd had enough of bridges, too. "But there's one thing I'm sure I can find."

"What's that?"

"Somewhere to eat!"

The café, when they found one to meet Patrick's requirements – namely, that it sold waffles – was in Wollestraat. It was long and narrow and surprisingly light, and the waitress was patient even when Patrick couldn't decide.

"We can always come back," said Roger. "We don't go home till Friday."

That settled it. Patrick would have waffles with strawberries and cream. Roger ordered a pancake with ice cream and raspberry sauce.

"This is delicious," he said, after a mouthful.

Patrick, devouring his waffle, just nodded.

Eventually, they tore themselves away, and wandered around the centre, looking at the lace shops and the craft shops and the chocolatiers.

"Mmm," murmured Patrick, looking at a tempting display of Belgian chocolates.

"We'll get some before we go home," Roger promised, smiling at Patrick's enthusiasm.

"It was a good idea, wasn't it? Coming here?"

"Yes, of course it was."

"I just thought ..."

"We could get things in perspective?" Roger teased gently, waiting for Patrick to see – quite literally – the joke.

Patrick smiled. "Yeah." He, too, had seen the trio of buildings that defied conventional lines and symmetry. He wondered if they'd been built at different times, or if they'd just settled differently. Certainly, if you painted them the way they were, most people would assume you'd failed to capture them accurately.

"Shall we go back?" said Roger.

"You know I love you?" said Patrick afterwards, as they lay curled together on the double bed.

"For better, for worse ..." Roger said lightly.

"For better, for worse ..." Patrick repeated as he rested his head on Roger's chest, unable to continue. There had been a time when they used to say the next few lines, but things had been difficult lately. Maybe the holiday would help. Things had been difficult the last time they'd come to Bruges, too ...

"What shall we do tomorrow?" asked Patrick.

"Climb the bell tower?"

Patrick laughed. "How many steps are there?"

"Three hundred and sixty-six."

"Oh, yes. I remember wondering whether it was chance or if there really was a step for every day."

"The view was spectacular," said Roger.

"It reminded me of Italy. I hadn't expected all those red roofs."

"And d'you remember the bells?"

Patrick smiled. "I was deaf for the rest of the day! It was your idea we went up just before noon."

"I didn't think."

"Neither did I."

"Why don't you go up?" suggested Roger. "I'll wait for you in the square."

"I'm not sure I could manage it now. Besides, we've got the pictures from last time."

"Mmm."

Patrick picked up the guide book to Bruges. " 'Canals were built connecting Bruges to Zeebrugge, Ostend and its old rival, Ghent,' " he read. " 'When the River Zwin silted up in the 15th century, the merchants decamped to Antwerp, but recently Flanders' former capital has witnessed a revival in its fortunes, attracting more than two million visitors each year.' If the weather's nice, we could go on a boat trip along the canals," he suggested. "And if it's wet, maybe a museum. Or we could buy some souvenirs. Your mother asked if we could get her some more lacework, and I'd like to get something for my sister." When there was no response, he glanced at Roger. Roger was asleep.

For a while, Patrick lay still. Then, when a tear dropped on to Roger's hairless chest, he brushed a hand across his eyes, and, very quietly, got up and went into the bathroom.

The next day was the sort you dreamed about: clear and bright, the sun pleasantly warm, the air invigorating. As they walked through the town – technically it was a city – Roger thought again how much it reminded him of both Venice and Amsterdam, although that was to detract from Bruges in its own right. True, it was old and had canals, and, like Amsterdam, hordes of cyclists on old-fashioned bikes – none of your state-of-the-art cycles and helmets here – but life seemed less hectic. The locals were tall and stylish like Italians – or perhaps they were Italians as there were many overseas visitors wandering up and down the cobbled streets.

They had to queue for a little while, but soon they were sitting in one of the boats which took tourists along the city's canals. Their guide, who was also responsible for steering, cast off, and they pulled away from the small jetty, watched by those waiting for the next boat.

They smiled as they realised that, at last, they'd found the bridge they'd spent much of the previous afternoon searching for. Many of the stone bridges they saw were several centuries old, some too low for their boat to pass under. The arches touched their own reflections to become ovals in the water. They passed a former hospital (the building had once been the British Embassy but was now a nursery school), and a museum which housed paintings by Flemish artists. Some of the houses had lattice windows, which overhung the canals, and many had ornate gables.

"What now?" asked Roger, after the guide had helped them off.

"Let's have a hot drink, indoors somewhere." He'd noticed Roger shiver as they passed along a shady part of the canal. Out of the sun, it could be quite cold, and here, near the water, damp. Roger had had a bad chill a few months earlier, and Patrick was still worried about him. He tried to mask his concern by adding lightly, "Maybe we'll find somewhere that does pancakes, too."

They stopped at one of the cafes surrounding a large cobbled square. From a glassed-in terrace, they watched the tourists milling about, and felt pleasantly idle.

"I could sit here all day," said Roger, more relaxed than he had been in a long time.

As they strolled through the town, Roger felt again the desire to link arms with Patrick, but he didn't know the law and customs of this foreign city. Would they just look faintly ridiculous, a couple of middle-aged queers? Bruges felt safe, full as it was of tourists and students, but it took only one person to object to their sexuality and the holiday would be spoiled. It was easier to let it go.

They spent several hours just looking around. They wandered down alleys, each of which seemed to lead them back to a canal or to one of the squares with its intricately carved buildings, the architecture of the newer ones blending in with that of the old. They tried to interpret Flemish street names. And they arrived unexpectedly at the white walled Beguinage, still used as a convent, its lawn bright with yellow daffodils. Nearby, on the grassy area between the canal and the street where carriages waited, a pair of swans preened themselves. Roger remembered hearing a long time before that swans mated for life. He'd wondered then what their secret was.

Later that afternoon, they sat outside enjoying the spring weather and lingering over a cup of strong coffee which, as usual, was served along with a small rich chocolate. On one side of the market square, striped umbrellas – some red and yellow, some green and yellow – made a bold splash of colour against the grey of the cobblestones.

The sun was warm on Roger's bare head. He was glad he'd gone bald, although, if it stayed warm, perhaps he'd have to think about buying a hat. He'd never really liked his bright red hair, and hadn't minded losing it. Funny, Patrick said that was one of the first things that had attracted him, his hair. He knew other people had always noticed it, too, but it had made him feel conspicuous.

"D'you think this is the same café as all those years ago?" asked Patrick softly.

"Maybe," Roger replied, his mind drifting. All those years ago ...

It was all going too fast for him. The decision to buy a house together, the visit to the building society to arrange a mortgage, letting their family and friends know ... He wanted to tell Patrick to slow down, that it was too much, too soon, but he was on a roller-coaster and couldn't get off. His love for Patrick was being worn down, trampled, suffocated by everyday routine.

Eventually he couldn't take any more, and stayed out until four in the morning. He slept in the spare room – well, spent the night there, his body still tingling. For months he'd tried to find the right words to tell Patrick he was leaving. He couldn't take the commitment involved, the responsibility, the feeling he'd been backed into a corner.

And then, suddenly, everything slipped into place. His certainty about what he wanted from life, his confidence that he was doing the right thing, his love for Patrick. He'd come through some sort of identity crisis and was the stronger for it.

It was the only time he'd ever been unfaithful to Patrick.

He looked across at his partner, who'd been waiting patiently, and smiled.

Patrick glanced down at the table, then looked up into Roger's eyes. "I'm glad you stayed. I wouldn't have wanted you to go."

For a while, neither spoke. Then Patrick continued.

"I knew I'd pushed too hard. I needed you so much, you see. I didn't know what to do. So I just waited." He stopped and swallowed. "Whatever happened, it doesn't matter." In his eyes, there was both understanding and compassion.

Roger had always wondered if Patrick had guessed. He wondered why his partner had to tell him now, just when thoughts of leaving him were again uppermost in his mind. He loved Patrick, but sometimes love just wasn't enough.

They lapsed into an undemanding silence, punctuated every once in a while by the sound of hooves as a horse-drawn carriage passed by.

The days passed quickly. For Roger, it was a relief when the film in their camera ran out; now he could relax and not have to think whether a particular view would make a good photo. True, they could buy some more film, in fact Patrick had wanted to, but Roger persuaded him against it. A genial American tourist had already taken a picture of them standing next to each other in front of the Town Hall.

"We've got enough photos," Roger said. For a split second, he glimpsed the anguish in Patrick's eyes, then it was gone.

While they walked along Zuidzandstraat, a white balloon had come sailing towards them. Smiling, Patrick had managed to catch it, and together they took it back to the little boy who'd accidentally let go of its string. The mother had been inordinately grateful, and had tried to thank them in English once she'd realised they were foreigners. They'd smiled and shrugged and nodded, too, and accepted one of the sweets the child had held out.

They finished their shopping. The sky was grey now, and it had turned cold. Tired of sight-seeing, they went straight back to their hotel. This time tomorrow they'd be on the ferry heading for Dover.

Patrick now lay asleep on the bed, while Roger quietly packed some of their things. Patrick had had a bad night. Roger, who didn't sleep much these days, had heard him tossing and turning. The last few days had been a well-needed breathing-space for both of them, but they'd known it couldn't last. It was time to go home.

Suddenly overwhelmed by emotion, Roger sat down on the edge of the bed, careful not to disturb Patrick. The fear was back again, fear of what was to come. It had haunted him, haunted them both for the past two years, ever since the doctor had confirmed what Roger already suspected. He'd undergone the treatment they'd recommended, but the specialist had warned him at the outset that they might not have caught it in time. Now there was nothing more they could do. He loved Patrick with all his heart, but it no longer made any difference. The cancer was only in remission. This would be their last time in Bruges.

THE END

Also Available from BeWrite Books

Crime

Sweet Molly Maguire – Terry Houston

The surreal world of a mean city newspaper swallowed the very toughest or spat them out. This circus of hopeless drunks and heartless back-stabbers was no place for Sweet Molly Maguire. She died, raped and pregnant, and didn't merit a single line of print. But for one reporter, her death wasn't the end of just another story. It was the opening sentence in a search for something rare in the news room … the bitter truth.

Paperback ISBN 1-904224-05-9
$13.50 US/ £9.80 UK/ $21.24 Canada/ €15.55 Europe
Ebook ISBN 1-904224-01-6
$6.55 US/ £4.80 UK/ $10.40 Canada/ €7.65 Europe
CD – Rom ISBN 1-904224-06-7
$10.25 US/ £7.50 UK/ $16.25 Canada/ €11.90 Europe

Horror

Chill – Terri Pine, Peter Lee, Andrew Müller

Dim the lights. Tug up the quilt so that only your eyes are visible. Now, slip into the dark, dark night of this world's greatest masters of macabre. Try not to sleep. Watch for moving shadows. And – whatever happens – *don*□ get out of bed … you may catch your very death …

Paperback ISBN 1-904224-08-3
$13.50 US/ £9.80 UK/ $21.24 Canada/ €15.55 Europe
Ebook ISBN 1-904224-03-2
$6.55 US/ £4.80 UK/ $10.40 Canada/ €7.65 Europe
CD – Rom ISBN 1-904224-11-3
$10.25 US/ £7.50 UK/ $16.25 Canada/ €11.90 Europe

Crime

Marks – Sam Smith

George Hawkins is a small town detective – low on ambition, lower on glamour. The most exciting part of life is making midnight chalk marks on tyres and roads ... when the marks still match up the following morning, he has proof that someone's been playing away from home. But George's humdrum life is turned upside down within a single day when he witnesses a hit-and-run, his house is burgled, and his girlfriend disappears, leaving him prime suspect.

Paperback ISBN 1-904224-09-1
$13.50 US/ £9.80 UK/ $21.24 Canada/ €15.55 Europe
Ebook ISBN 1-904224-02-4
$6.55 US/ £4.80 UK/ $10.40 Canada/ €7.65 Europe
CD – Rom ISBN 1-904224-17-2
$10.25 US/ £7.50 UK/ $16.25 Canada/ €11.90 Europe

Autobiography

The Golden Locket – A Post-Edwardian Childhood – Dorothy Kathleen Kirby

It may not have mattered to Dorothy Kathleen Kirby that she didn't live to see the book she had written. She had *lived* the memories between its covers. In nine decades that saw the Flanders trenches and the terror attack on Manhattan, Dorothy focused on the simple detail of everyday life, and discovered a wonderful world. Page by delightful page, you cannot help but be struck by the truth that counting blessings one by one can produce a mighty sum.

Paperback ISBN 1-904224-07-5
$13.50 US/ £9.80 UK/ $21.24 Canada/ €15.55 Europe
Ebook ISBN 1-904224-00-8
$6.55 US/ £4.80 UK/ $10.40 Canada/ €7.65 Europe
CD – Rom ISBN 1-904224-10-5
$10.25 US/ £7.50 UK/ $16.25 Canada/ €11.90 Europe

Crime

The Knotted Cord – Alistair Kinnon

The body of a naked young boy hanging in a dusty barn stirs sickening feelings of déjà vu in the detective. As he untangles each knot in the tangled cord of his investigation, he uncovers a murderous thread ... and police prejudices which may have allowed previous killings to happen ... not to mention his own guilt! **Alistair Kinnon** has written much more than a tense, psychological crime novel -- his twisting plot takes the reader into the murky world of child sex-for-sale … the parent's darkest nightmare and the child's greatest threat.

Paperback ISBN 1-904224-12-1
$13.50 US/ £9.80 UK/ $21.24 Canada/ €15.55 Europe
Ebook ISBN 1-904224-04-1
$6.55 US/ £4.80 UK/ $10.40 Canada/ €7.65 Europe
CD – Rom ISBN 1-904224-13-X
$10.25 US/ £7.50 UK/ $16.25 Canada/ €11.90 Europe

Fantasy Humour

Zolin – A Rockin' Good Wizard – Barry Ireland

Worlds go along happily side-by-side in their own dimensiverses … until they accidentally bump into each other. Then a wild Glasgow rock band, randy witches, dragons for hire and kings and queens end up rocking where they should have been rolling. And bewildered apprentice wizard, Zolin, is piggy in the middle. **Barry Ireland's** book is to Fantasy what The Hitchhiker's Guide to the Galaxy was to Sci Fi. An adult fairy tale!

Paperback ISBN 1-904224-19-9
$13.50 US/ £9.80 UK/ $21.24 Canada/ €15.55 Europe
Ebook ISBN 1-904224-18-0
$6.55 US/ £4.80 UK/ $10.40 Canada/ €7.65 Europe
CD – Rom ISBN 1-904224-20-2
$10.25 US/ £7.50 UK/ $16.25 Canada/ €11.90 Europe

Coming Soon
Porlock Counterpoint – Sam Smith
The Fat Moon Dance – Elizabeth Taylor
Spartacus Thorn – Dazz Jackson
Kitchen Sink Concert – Ishbel Moore
Rules Of The Hunt – Hugh McCracken

N.B The price for paperback and CD-Rom excludes postage and packaging.

All the above titles are available from

www.bewrite.net

Printed in the United Kingdom
by Lightning Source UK Ltd.
115759UKS00001B/13

9 781904 224402